PIANO

Jean Echenoz was born in Provence in 1947. He studied organic chemistry in Lille and then double bass in Metz before he turned to writing. He is one of the most influential French writers of his generation. He won the Prix Goncourt for his novel *I'm Off*.

Jean Echenoz

PIANO

TRANSLATED FROM THE FRENCH BY
Mark Polizzotti

VINTAGE

Published by Vintage 2005

2 4 6 8 10 9 7 5 3 1

First published with the title *Au piano* by
Les Éditions de Minuit in 2003

First published in Great Britain in 2004 by The Harvill Press

Vintage
Random House, 20 Vauxhall Bridge Road, London SW1V 2SA

Random House Australia (Pty) Limited
20 Alfred Street, Milsons Point, Sydney
New South Wales 2061, Australia

Random House New Zealand Limited
18 Poland Road, Glenfield, Auckland 10, New Zealand

Random House (Pty) Limited
Isle of Houghton, Corner Boundary Road & Carse O'Gowrie,
Houghton, 2198, South Africa

The Random House Group Limited Reg. No. 954009
www.randomhouse.co.uk/vintage

A CIP catalogue record for this book
is available from the British Library

This book is supported by the French Ministry for Foreign Affairs, as part
of the Burgess programme headed for the French Embassy in London by the
Institut Français du Royaume-Uni

Liberté • Égalité • Fraternité
RÉPUBLIQUE FRANÇAISE

ISBN 0 09 946943 X

Printed and bound in Great Britain by
Cox & Wyman Limited, Reading, Berkshire

I

ONE

TWO MEN APPEAR at the end of Boulevard de Courcelles, coming from the direction of Rue de Rome.

One, slightly taller than average, says nothing. Under a large, light-coloured raincoat buttoned to the neck, he is wearing a black suit with a black bow tie. Small cufflinks set in onyx-quartz punctuate his immaculate wrists. He is, in short, very well dressed, though his pallid face and gaping eyes suggest a worried frame of mind. His white hair is brushed back. He is afraid. He is going to die a violent death in twenty-two days' time but—as he is yet unaware of this—that is not what he is afraid of.

The man accompanying him is the complete opposite in appearance: younger, considerably shorter, small, garrulous, and smiling too much; wearing a small brown-and-tan checked hat, a pair of trousers faded in patches, and a formless sweater with nothing underneath. His feet are clad in moccasins marbled with damp spots.

"Nice hat," the well-dressed man finally observes as they are about to reach the gates of Parc Monceau. These are the first words he has spoken in an hour.

"Really?" worries the other. "It's useful, in any case, that's a fact, but aesthetically speaking I'm not quite sure what to make of it. It's salvage, you understand. I wouldn't have bought it myself."

"No, no," the elegant one protests. "It's nice."

"My stepson found it on the train," the other replies. "Someone must have forgotten it. But it was too small for him, you see, my stepson has an extremely large skull, not to mention an enormous IQ. But it's just my size, which doesn't mean that I'm not any more foolish—I mean, that I'm any more foolish—than the next man. How about a walk in the park?"

On either side of the rotunda where the park's watchmen were on guard, the monumental gilded cast-iron portals stood open. The two men passed through them and entered the park and, for a moment, the younger one seemed to hesitate as to which direction to take. He masked his hesitation by talking nonstop, as if his sole reason for being there was to distract his companion, to try to make him forget his fear. And this was indeed his role. But although he performed it conscientiously, he didn't always seem to enjoy complete success. Before arriving at the park, he had explored various topics of a political, cultural, or sexual nature, without his monologue triggering the slightest exchange, without any of it blossoming into conversation. From the park entrance, he cast a distrustful gaze all around, from the

Virginia tulips to the Japanese loquat trees: waterfall, rocks, lawns. The other man seemed to look at nothing but his own internal terror.

The other man, whose name was Max Delmarc, was some fifty years of age. Although his income was quite respectable, and although he was famous in the eyes of a good million or so people and had for the past twenty years undergone all sorts of psychological and chemical treatments, he was, as we said, dying of fright. When the feeling enveloped him to this extent, he would normally fall completely silent. But now here he was, opening his mouth.

"I'm thirsty, Bernie," said Max. "I feel a bit thirsty. Supposing we stop by your place?"

Bernie looked at him gravely. "I think it would be better if we didn't, Monsieur Max," he said. "Monsieur Parisy wouldn't be very happy. And you remember what happened last time."

"Come on," Max insisted, "you're two minutes away from here. Just one little drink."

"No," Bernie said, "no, but I can call Monsieur Parisy if you like. We can ask him."

"Fine," Max surrendered. "Forget it."

Then, noticing a kiosk to the left selling waffles, cold drinks, and skipping ropes, he walked briskly in its direction. Bernie, having followed, passed, and preceded him towards the menu displayed near the cash register, quickly glanced over the list before Max could catch up—no alcohol, all's well.

"Would you like some coffee, Monsieur Max?"

"No," answered Max, disappointed by his own perusal of the menu, "that's O.K."

They started walking again. They passed in front of the bust of Guy de Maupassant hovering over a girl, then, on the other side of the lawn, a statue of Ambroise Thomas accompanied by another girl and, farther to the east, Edouard Pailleron towering above still another girl in a fainting fit. In this park, apparently, the statues of great men feared being alone, for each of them had a young woman at his feet. And better still, just after the waterfall, no fewer than three female companions—one of whom had lost both her arms—surrounded Charles Gounod. But Bernie preferred that they avoid passing the composer's memorial. Worse than that, from farther away he spotted, close by the children's play area, the monument to Frédéric Chopin: good God almighty, Bernie said to himself, Chopin. Especially not Chopin. He changed course abruptly, forcing Max to make an about-turn and diverting his attention by praising the variety, abundance, and polychromy of the flora, pointing out the great age of the sycamore maple and the substantial circumference of the Oriental plane tree.

"Look, just look at them, Monsieur Max, look how beautiful it is," his voice filled with emotion. "The world is beautiful. The world is beautiful, don't you think so?" Neither slowing his step nor answering the question, Max pretended to grant this world a look and lightly shrugged his shoulders. "All right," Bernie conceded sheepishly, "fine. But at least agree that it's very well lit."

After dragging Max through every corner of the park, other than the area around Chopin; after trying to make him admire the oval basin, the pyramid with its pyramidion; and after secretly glancing at his watch, Bernie inflected their path towards a park exit, taking Allée de la Comtesse de Ségur, along which sat Alfred de Musset. No problem with Musset, except that the right arm was also missing from the young creature who, leaning over him, rested her left hand on Alfred's left shoulder.

It was seven thirty-five p.m., a hesitant late spring, but the sun was still present. Their faces directed towards its imminent setting, heading west on Avenue Van Dyck, the two men left the park. Since his attempt to procure a drink, Max had not unclenched his teeth, while Bernie, playing his part diligently, did not stop talking or watching him. Max had not left his side except for two or three minutes, just long enough to discreetly go and vomit from fear behind a Hungarian oak. As he had already vomited twice that afternoon, all that came up was bile in a series of highly painful heaves. Now, outside the park, they walked up a service road of Avenue Hoche, taking the first turn on the right—at the corner of which stood a bar, where Max tried once more to entice Bernie in and Bernie silently refused—then a few more yards and there it was, number 252. They were here.

They went in. Stairways, hallways, passageways, doorways that they opened and shut until they reached a dark space littered with cables, pulleys, large open cases, and displaced furniture. In the air floated the noise of a swell or a crowd. It was now eight-thirty on the dot. Max had just removed his overcoat and suddenly, just when he least expected it, Bernie shoved him from behind through a curtain, the swell was immediately transformed into a tempest, and there it was—the piano.

There it was, the terrible Steinway with its wide white keyboard ready to devour you, those monstrous teeth that would chew you up with the full width of its ivories and all its enamel, waiting to mash you into a pulp. Almost stumbling from Bernie's push, Max just managed to keep his balance. Drowning in the torrent of applause from the packed auditorium that had stood to welcome him, he lurched, short of breath, towards the fifty-two teeth. He sat before them, the conductor brandished his baton, silence immediately fell, and they were off. I really can't take this any more. This is no kind of life. Although, let's face it, I could have been born in Manila and ended up selling loose cigarettes, or a shoe-shine boy in Bogotá, a diver in Decazeville. Might as well get on with it, then, since we're here. First movement, *maestoso*, of the Second Concerto in F-minor, Op. 21, by Frédéric Chopin.

TWO

FROM THE AUDIENCE, even from the front row, no-one can imagine how hard it is. It seems to happen all by itself.

And in fact, for Max, things do begin moving by themselves. Once the orchestra has embarked on the long overture, he starts to calm down. Then, on cue, as soon as he enters into the movement, everything seems better. His fears subside after a few bars, then fade away with the first wrong note—a good wrong note, in a rapid passage. The kind of mistake that passes by overlooked. At this point, Max becomes liberated. Now he has the situation in hand, he can stroll around, he is in his element. Every half-tone speaks to him, every pause is right, the series of chords touch down like dancing birds, he would like it never to stop, but already it's the end of the first movement. Pause. Everyone has his little cough while waiting for the next one to begin, you rake your throat, you expel the mucus from your polluted lungs, everyone clears his windpipe as best he can and then up starts the second movement, *larghetto:* slow, meditative, extremely exposed, no room for mistakes, and Max doesn't make any; it comes off as easy as pie. You cough some more, then it's the third, an elegant *allegro vivace,* just watch me hand you this one on a platter—ouch, a second false note at around bar 200. I always slip at the same place in the finale, but there again it's lost in the rush. They haven't noticed a thing. We're getting there, we're almost through, chromatic descent and rise, then four punctuations by the orchestra, two concluding chords, and there you go, it's in the bag, bravo, goodnight, bravo, curtain, bravo, no encores, end of story.

Tingling with fatigue but having forgotten all about his stage fright, Max went up to his dressing room, which was flooded in bouquets. "What is it with all these flowers?" he groused. "You know damn well I can't deal with them, chuck them out for me."

"Right away," said Bernie, who gathered up the offending bouquets *presto agitato* and slipped out, loaded down like a hearse. Max fell on to a chair in front of an untidy console-table dominated by a mirror, in the depths of which, in shadow, Parisy was mopping his neck with a rolled-up ball of Kleenex.

"Ah," Max said without turning around, preparing to unbutton his shirt, "there you are."

"That was excellent," beamed the impresario.

"I know," said Max, "I thought so too. But I don't really feel like playing that thing again, I know it too well. And besides, the orchestra part's pretty weak when you get down to it, you can tell Chopin wasn't too good at that. Anyway, I'm rather fed up with orchestras in general." As he undid his top button, it jumped off his shirt and took refuge in the mess on the console-table.

"Anyway," Parisy said, approaching, "you don't have anything but recitals until summer. You know—Berlin."

Still not turning around, searching for the fugitive button, Max watched the mirror amplify Parisy's massive and balding silhouette, the physique of retractive Turkish delight with thick glasses, check-patterned suit, chronic perspiration, and voice of a light tenor. "Remind me what the programme is," said Max.

"O.K., so you've got Nantes at the end of the week," Parisy warbled. "You have the recital at Salle Gaveau on the nineteenth, then nothing until that business on TV. And then Japan called again, they want to know when you can get back to recording the complete Chausson, they need a date so they can book Cerumen."

"I need time," said Max. "I'm not ready."

"What I mean is, they need to know very soon," Parisy emphasised, "they have to plan their schedule."

"I need time," Max repeated. "I'm dying of thirst. Where's the kid?"

The kid had returned, minus the flowers. He was standing by the door, waiting for someone to give him something to do.

"I wouldn't mind a drink, Bernie," Max indicated, still without turning around, while finally snaring the errant button between two empty vases. Bernie opened a cabinet and pulled out a glass and a bottle. After clearing off a corner of the console-table, he set them on a tray in front of Max.

"I'll be back," said Bernie. "I'm going to Janine's to get some ice."

Without waiting for its arrival, Max filled his glass four-fifths full under the reticent eye of his manager, still framed close-up in the mirror. "Don't go on at me, Parisy, if you don't mind. We agreed that I'm allowed after a concert. Beforehand, fine, no problem, but afterwards I'm allowed."

"That's not really it," Parisy qualified, "it's just that you haven't left much room for the ice."

"Right you are," said Max, emptying half his glass in one gulp. "See? Now there's room."

Parisy shook his head, searching his pocket for a new Kleenex, and grimaced when he noticed it was the last. He crumpled the packet and tossed it towards a wastepaper-basket as Bernie re-emerged, carrying an insulated yellow-and-white ice bucket. "Thanks, Bernie, no, no, I don't need the tongs. On the contrary." Max plunged two ice cubes into his glass before running a third cube over his forehead, temples, and neck; then, continuing to address Parisy in the mirror: "Where would I be without Bernie?"

"Good, good," the impresario approved vaguely.

"While we're on the subject," Bernie timidly intervened.

"What?" said Parisy.

"Well, the thing is," said Bernie. "I'm afraid I'm forced to ask you, if it's possible, of course, for a small rise."

"Absolutely out of the question," Parisy said stiffly.

"It's just that I have expenses," Bernie elaborated. "For instance, I have a stepson who's very intelligent, I have to help finance his studies. He has a very high IQ, you see, I have to send him to the top schools, which means private lessons, which are very expensive."

"Crap," decreed Parisy.

"Moreover, keep in mind," stressed Bernie, "that my role is very delicate. I have to assist Monsieur Max in all kinds of situations, watch over his diet," (Max smiled at these words) "buck him up when he doesn't feel like playing. That all makes for a heavy responsibility. And besides," he impressed upon them, "pushing him on-stage every evening isn't always easy. Sometimes he fights back. Monsieur Max is an artist," Bernie concluded. "He owes himself to his public, and please understand that in a certain way all of this happens through me."

"You must be joking," said Parisy.

"Pardon me," Max broke in, "but I completely support the kid's request. He's indispensable to me and I won't take responsibility if I don't have him."

A soaked Parisy squeezed out his Kleenex, looked for another one before remembering that there weren't any, then used his sleeve to dry his forehead. "I'll have to think about it," he said. "We'll have to talk about it."

"Why don't we talk about it now?" asked Bernie.

"Absolutely," Max instigated, "why put it off?"

"Let's have a seat, then," sighed Parisy, pulling from his pocket a small rectangular object, like a mobile phone or electric razor.

"With pleasure," said Bernie as Max emptied his glass and stood up.

"Well," he said, "I'll let the two of you work it out."

When he left the dressing room, Parisy had just pushed a button located at the end of the rectangular object, which turned out to be a small, battery-operated portable fan, whose rattling click Max could hear all the way to the end of the hall.

THREE

WHEN MAX GOT HOME from Salle Pleyel, Alice displayed little reaction, which was not surprising given that she was already asleep. She and Max occupied two large floors in the eighteenth *arrondissement*, near Château-Rouge—large enough so that each of them could live and work there in complete independence, she upstairs and he downstairs, without seeing each other from one day's end to the next if they didn't want to.

Max closed the entrance door softly before going into his studio: a grand piano; a small desk; a very small fridge, the kind you find in hotel rooms; shelves full of musical scores; and a divan. That was where he spent most of his time, linked to the upper floor of the maisonette by an intercom, protected from the bustle of the street by two double-glazed windows. As everything was well insulated for sound, Max could make as much noise as he wanted without the danger of waking Alice and, once he had taken something to drink from the refrigerator, he lifted the fall board of the piano. Setting his glass on the instrument, he stared at the keyboard. It wouldn't have been a bad idea to revisit the evening's two blunders, to isolate those passages, study them, take them apart like little watches, two little mechanisms that you could then piece back together after identifying the damage, repairing the defective gear for next time. But then again, I've really had enough of this concerto. And besides, I'm tired.

So he might as well take a shower, then go back into the studio, pick up his glass, and carry it into the bedroom. Once in bed, Max nonetheless thought some more about his two wrong notes, at the beginning of the first movement and in the second third of the third. It wasn't serious; they weren't bad wrong notes. To muff a note, or even a chord, is inconsequential when it's buried in a huge cascade. In those cases it passes all by itself in the flood, and no-one notices. It would have been more troublesome to have erred on a passage in the second movement, which is less dense, more fragile and more naked; everyone might have heard it. But anyway, enough of that. Instead, think about Rose for a moment, as you do every night. And besides, you've had enough to drink as it is; nobody's forcing you to empty that glass. It's late, let's turn off the light. Good. O.K., now go to sleep. What, it's not working? O.K., fine, take the pill. With a glass of water. I said water. There.

The pill took effect after twenty minutes, and twenty more minutes later sleep became paradoxical: for a handful of seconds, an inconsequential dream agitated Max's brain while his eyes also fidgeted rapidly beneath his lids. Then he woke up earlier than he would have liked and tried to fall back asleep, but in vain: keeping his eyelids shut without managing to reach a true state of wakefulness, he was beset by absurd ideas, shaky reasonings, pointless lists, and endless calculations, with brief dips back into sleep, but all too brief.

Right, now get up, it's after ten. Come on now. Fine, all right, not just yet, but certainly no later than ten-thirty. Sure, go ahead, then, think about Rose all you want. Doubt it'll do you any good, but that's your business.

FOUR

THE STORY OF ROSE goes back to his days at the conservatory in Toulouse, something like thirty years ago. In her final year of cello classes and endowed with supernatural beauty, Rose owned a white Fiat that was a little too large for her. Every day she emerged from it at the same time in front of the same café where, always at the same terrace table, she spoke only with the same bearded and rather fierce-looking individual who (to cut to the chase) didn't appear to be her boyfriend. Every day she was more incredibly beautiful, even if one could perhaps object to a single detail, her nose, which was slightly too hooked. On the other hand, that only made her more attractive: it was the nose of an Egyptian empress, a Spanish aristocrat, or a bird of prey—in short, a real nose. For that entire year, Max had contrived to be seated every day at the same time and at the same café as she, but at another table, neither too far nor too near, from which he watched Rose without daring to speak to her—too good for me too good for me, what in God's name can they be talking about?

Only once had Max taken the plunge and sat at a table next to hers. She asked him for a light, which might be considered an advance, perhaps even an encouragement, but that's just it: it was such a predictable advance, so conventional an encouragement that it wasn't worthy of such a supernatural beauty. It was disrespectful even to have entertained such a hypothesis, forget all that forget all that. So Max handed her his lighter with a detached gesture, painstakingly indifferent, without the spark from the lighter igniting the least speck of powder, and that's where they left it. After that he continued to look at her as she looked elsewhere, without letting himself be too noticed by her, not taking his eyes off her but always with the utmost discretion. Or so he thought. Then, when summer came, Rose left town for the holidays and the cello behind for good. A vacant Max in abandoned Toulouse went to have a drink at the same outdoor café, also empty, where only a few patrons were to be found—mainly tourists, but also, what do you know, the fierce bearded fellow, with whom Max struck up a conversation.

It didn't take long for the talk to turn to Rose. Mouth agape, Max soon learned that it was about him that they had talked. It was Max himself they discussed, she going on about him non-stop, to the point where the bearded chap sometimes had to suggest she sing a different tune for a change. It turned out that Rose hadn't dared approach Max any more than Max Rose, the latter having only once ventured to ask him for a light. And worse still, according to this fellow, the only reason Rose frequented this café every day was that she hoped to see Max, believing that he was a regular there. At this news, Max remained frozen, in arrest, in apnoea, remembering only after a minute that man needs to breathe, to inhale some air, especially when he's overcome by an enormous desire to weep. But where is she now, he pleaded, how can I find her, is there an address where she can be reached? Well, no, the other answered, she's gone now, her studies are over and she moved to God knows where.

Since then, Max had spent a good part of his life expecting, hoping, waiting to run into her by chance. Not a day went by without his thinking about it for a few seconds, a few minutes, or more. Now this isn't entirely rational. After thirty years, Rose could have been living on the other side of the world, already having, according to his informant, some predisposition in that direction. Or perhaps she was even dead, having had, on that score, no less predisposition than the rest of us.

FIVE

UP AT TEN-THIRTY, Max discovered his half-full glass next to the bed, went to empty it in the sink, and then, standing naked in the kitchen, made some coffee.

He would wash up only at the end of the day, before going out to perform or see friends. For now he donned soft, practical, fairly ample garments, such as a sweatsuit or an old wrinkled beige linen shirt and canvas trousers that were no longer very white. Moreover, it seemed that, these days, all his buttons were dropping off one by one; his shirts had lived full lives and showed it. Two or three times a week lately, at the slightest excuse, whether through overly zealous washing or ironing by the cleaning woman or washing machine, muscle stretch, awkward movement, or spontaneous decay, a worn thread would give way, the button would leave its mooring and fall like a dead leaf, ripe fruit, or dry acorn, bouncing and rolling protractedly on the ground.

Then it's the same daily routine: after coffee, piano. The time is long past since Max did exercises before getting down to business, scales and arpeggios serving only to loosen up his fingers before a concert, like limbering-up exercises to gently warm the muscles. He works directly on the pieces that he will soon have to perform, polishing up a few phrases of his own invention, ruses and technical manoeuvres adapted to such-and-such an obstacle, for three or four hours at a stretch. He sits at his keyboard in a feverish mix of excitement, discouragement, and anxiety, although after a while anxiety gains the upper hand. At first lodged in the pit of his plexus, it then invades the surrounding areas, mainly Max's stomach in an increasingly oppressive, convulsive, and pitiless way, until, mutating at around one-thirty from the psychic to the somatic, this anxiety metamorphoses into hunger.

In the kitchen, Max now searched through the refrigerator for viable solutions but, as Alice had done no shopping, nothing stood out with sufficient conviction to sate this hunger on its own. Which was so much the better, since eating at home alone isn't exactly a thrilling prospect; anxiety can then overtake hunger to the point of eliminating it, preventing you from eating, while the hunger, for its part, grows larger and larger—it's terrible. As usual, then, Max went out to eat in the neighbourhood, where the ethnic brew had fermented into a proliferation of African, Tunisian, Laotian, Lebanese, Indian, Portuguese, Balkan, and Chinese restaurants. There was also a decent Japanese that had just opened two blocks away. Japanese it is; Max slipped on a jacket and went out. He left his building, headed up the street, and there, reaching the corner, he ran into her. No, not Rose. Somebody else.

This somebody else, let's not mince words, was also a supernaturally beautiful woman. Not the same type as Rose, although, yes, perhaps there was something. Max had noticed her some time before, but he didn't know her, had never spoken to her, had never even exchanged a single glance or smile with her— although she apparently lived in Max's neighbourhood, maybe even on his street, perhaps only a few yards away. He had seen her off and on for years, who knows how many—maybe eight, ten, twelve years, or even more; he didn't remember when the first time was.

Always alone, she might be spotted twice in the same week, but months might also go by without Max seeing her once. She was a tall woman, touching and dark and gentle and tragic and profound and, once past these adjectives, which mainly applied to her smile and her eyes, Max would have had a devil of a time trying to describe her. But that smile, those eyes—tightly linked to each other, as if interdependent, and, to Max's great regret, never directed at him, being reserved for other privileged and unknown persons—were not the only attributes of hers that he found intriguing. There was also, in the midst of this lower-class, noisy, multi-coloured, and overall rather bleak and shabby neighbourhood, an extreme elegance in this woman's bearing—in her walk, her posture, her choice of clothing—that one could hardly imagine existing outside of the pretty, calm, rich neighbourhoods, and

23

maybe not even then. Anachronistic wasn't the word; anatopic would be the word, but it doesn't exist yet, at least not to Max's knowledge. For him, this unattainable creature was a kind of variation on the Rose theme, a repetition of the same motif. Meeting her in person, Max also tried to meet her gaze, managed to do so for only a fraction of a second without glimpsing any particular sign of interest on her part and two hundred yards farther on was the Japanese. Sushi or sashimi?

Sashimi, for a change. Then he returned home and sat down again at the piano, having no further reason to be out. Two or three times he had to answer the phone, which seldom rang to begin with, and which, as Max almost never called anybody, now rang even less. At around six he heard Alice come in, but that was no reason to interrupt his practising: he would spend the rest of the afternoon refining a few nuances of two movements, "Presentiment" followed by "Death", of *Piano Sonata 1.X.1905* by Janáček, after which he'd go up to find Alice busy in the kitchen. "Hmm," he'd say, "fish." "Yes," Alice would reply, "why?" "No reason," Max would say, setting the table, "I like fish. Where do you keep the fish forks?" Then they'd eat together, more or less telling each other about their day, and then they'd spend a moment in front of the television which that evening was showing *Artists and Models*—a film already familiar to Max, who interrupted its progress shortly after Dean Martin had lathered sun lotion on Dorothy Malone's shoulders while singing "Innamorata" to her. Then, each in their own room, they went to bed.

SIX

WITH A WEEK gone by since the concert at Salle Pleyel, Max still had some fifteen days to live, and one early morning he was speeding back to Paris in a TGV from Nantes where, the evening before, he had appeared on-stage at the Opéra Graslin with an all-Fauré programme. As usual, the terror of this recital had barely had time to fade from Max's body and mind when, at the prospect of performing again tonight at Salle Gaveau, a new panic had already taken hold of him. In an attempt to dilute it, to give himself something to do, Max left his seat and headed for the bar, unbalanced by the train's motion, grabbing headrests from behind.

He did not have to go very far to reach the bar, which at this hour was nearly empty. From here you could watch the country-side in peace, even though thick horizontal shafts across the mid-dles of the windows, incomprehensibly placed just at eye-level, forced you to bend down or crane up on tiptoe to enjoy said countryside, which wasn't very interesting to begin with. Having ordered a beer, Max reached into his pocket and pulled out a phone, on which he called a number.

"Hello," Parisy answered almost immediately, "how can I help you? Oh, it's you. So how did it go in Nantes?"

"Oh, not bad," Max replied, "but the hotel was a disgrace."

"Oh, right," said Parisy, his mind elsewhere, "I see."

"Listen, what were you thinking," Max asked, "getting me a room for the handicapped?"

Indeed: special bed and raised toilets, support bars attached to every wall, open-work seat in the bath, window with northern exposure overlooking a section of car park that (as symbols on the ground indicated) was also reserved for the disabled. The clinical-looking accommodation had nothing about it to brighten the mood of a man alone, especially of an artist alone, and more particularly of a terrified artist alone.

"I know," said Parisy, "I know, but there really wasn't anything else available. There must have been some kind of convention or something going on in Nantes, all the hotels were full."

"I understand," said Max, "but still."

"You know," Parisy went on, "that kind of room isn't all bad. It's much larger than the other kind, for instance. And did you notice, the doors are wider."

"Why wider?" asked Max.

"Because," Parisy explained, "they need to be big enough to fit two wheelchairs."

"Why two?" Max asked, surprised.

"Even the handicapped are entitled to love," pronounced Parisy.

"I understand," Max repeated, "but, well, really, there wasn't even a minibar."

"The handicapped are sober," Parisy remarked coldly.

"All right, fine," said Max, "whatever. Talk to you later."

And then, having downed his beer, he bought three little bottles of alcohol that he stuffed into his right pocket before returning to his seat.

In First Class, Smoking Section, Max had a group of four facing seats all to himself. One good thing about the TGV, at the time, was that in Car 13, First Class Smoking was next to the bar, which tended to make matters simpler. Coming from the Non-Smoking section, a man walked up to ask if one of the seats was free, adding that he wouldn't stay long, just long enough for one or two cigarettes. "Please," said Max with a gesture of hospitality, as if he were at home. While thanking him and producing cigarettes and a lighter, the man gave Max a slightly prolonged glance, making the latter wonder if the former had recognised him. After all, since his face sometimes appeared in newspapers and specialised magazines, on posters and record covers, it happened occasionally that people came up to talk to him—oddly enough, more often on public transport than anywhere else. It was never unpleasant, of course, even if sometimes embarrassing, but on this particular morning, in this particular train, Max, who was finding the time hanging heavy on his hands, wouldn't have minded a little conversation. But no: having incinerated his Marlboro, the other man suddenly went to sleep right there in front of him, mouth hanging open, and Max could clearly discern a dark filling in the upper right of his jaw. Oh well, so it goes, isn't that always the way. When you know you're a little famous, you're always a little more or a little less famous than you think, depending on the situation. So what shall I do with myself? Shrugging figurative shoulders, Max dug into his pocket for the first of the miniature liquor bottles.

Upon the train's arrival, well before it had come to a stop, the passengers stood up from their seats, retrieved their bags, and crowded around the doors. All except Max, who climbed down slowly from the carriage after everyone else. Bernie, who was waiting for him on Platform 8 at Montparnasse station, could see right away that all was not well. He rushed up and took Max's arm, labouring to stick to the straightest possible course towards the station exit while talking incessantly, informing the pianist that the reviews of the last Pleyel concert had been uniformly laudatory (anyway, that's what I heard, I never read the papers), that Gaveau would surely be packed tonight, that the States had called asking about a month-long tour, that the honorarium offered by the Fougères festival was scandalously unacceptable according to Parisy, and that, the complete Chausson being very much in demand, Japan was pressing them to know what date they should reserve for the Cerumen studios (couldn't they find something more inviting, as names go?), as well as a host of other things.

On the escalators, all this only provoked in Max knowing little snickers, which, in conjunction with the smell of his breath, made Bernie supremely nervous.

"By the way," said Max, "how did it go the other night with Parisy? You know, your rise."

"Well, actually, not badly," answered Bernie, "but it'll depend a bit on you."

"Never fear," said Max, tripping over a step, "it'll be fine. And if it's not fine, we'll get rid of him. You can always change managers. We make a good team, you and I, and Parisy is an idiot."

"Now really," Bernie objected.

"Shut up," Max ordered. "He doesn't know the first thing about music. He has the artistic sense of a yogurt. On top of which," he persisted, missing another step, "he's completely tone-deaf."

"Now really," Bernie repeated, gripping Max's elbow more firmly.

"He is, he is," Max developed. "He's so deaf that his ears are only good for holding up his glasses. And besides, he doesn't understand a thing about my project. But then again," he generalised, "no-one understands my project. Not even me."

As it was now twelve-something, after dropping Max off in front of his building in a taxi, Bernie walked down Boulevard

Barbès in search of a restaurant. He found one, ordered the daily special, and went downstairs where the telephone and toilets languished as usual. He used the latter, then picked up the former and dialled Parisy's number.

"So?" worried Parisy. "How is he?"

"Not too good," said Bernie. "I get the feeling he isn't too good."

"What!" exclaimed Parisy, "is he pissed again? This early already?"

"He's tired," Bernie allowed. "He looks really tired to me."

"Listen, Bernard," Parisy said sharply, "that's your problem, understood? It's your responsibility. You remember what we agreed the other day? I don't have to tell you that if the concert suffers for it, the deal's off. Go and do your duty now."

After Max had lunched at home at Château-Rouge, where Alice had left some cold chicken in the fridge, he dozed off a moment on the studio divan, was startled awake by the return of the fear that he tried to exorcise with a drink, managing only to potentiate it. When Bernie reappeared at his door late that afternoon to escort him to the concert as usual, Max looked even less sure of himself than he had at the station; Bernie had to guide him towards his shower before helping him get dressed. Then, at the corner of Rue Custine, he hailed a cab and they jumped in.

"Parc Monceau," Bernie announced.

"Parc Monceau again?" Max complained. "Why do you always take me there?"

"Parc Monceau is good," answered Bernie. "It's handy, it's pretty, it's easy to get to. It's near where I live. And anyway, it's all I could think of."

A dark grey sky hung over the boulevards filing past. The air was heavy with chilly gusts, little intermittent slaps that entered through the lowered windows of the taxi; Max was constantly opening and closing his raincoat. "Hey," he observed when the taxi pulled up in front of the gilded fence, "it's raining."

"Wait a minute before getting out," Bernie anticipated. "I'll cover you. And I'd like a receipt for that, please," he said to the driver before rushing around to the other side of the car, producing a telescopic umbrella. This he deployed above Max, who stumbled as he got out of the cab under the fine rain.

They again entered the park. Bernie had to contort himself somewhat to support Max by one arm while continuing to maintain, at the end of his other arm, the umbrella perfectly centred over Max's skull, as the latter protested, "Cover yourself, too, you're going to get soaked!"

"I've got my hat," Bernie reminded him.

"Listen," said Max, "suppose we go to your place instead and have a little drink, just one little beer, where it's nice and warm?"

"No, Monsieur Max," said Bernie in a firm voice.

"Listen," Max insisted, "you know the rain isn't good for my hands. It plays havoc with my fingers. I'm freezing, I feel my arthritis taking hold, I can feel it coming on. At this rate, I won't be able to play at all."

"Monsieur Max," Bernie moaned desperately.

Sensing his opponent falter, Max thrust a hand into a pocket of his raincoat, pulled out one of the miniatures bought on the TGV, and brandished it threateningly like a grenade. "Look at this," he said. "If this is what you're afraid of, I have some on me in any case. It can only warm me up. So here's the deal, it's very simple: either a beer at your place or I drink this right here. Would you prefer that?"

"This is not good," Bernie capitulated, "this is not good."

"*What's* not good?" Max persisted. "Where's the harm? And anyway, where'd you say your place was, exactly?"

"Rue Murillo," Bernie answered in a doleful voice, "just over that way."

"I know it well," said Max. "So hey," he snickered unpleasantly, "you live in a pretty fancy neighbourhood."

"It's tiny," Bernie protested limply. "It's on the top floor, just enough space for my stepson and me. It was in the family."

"Let's go," said Max.

A resigned Bernie followed more than led Max towards the park's south gate, still taking care, out of principle, to avoid the monument dedicated to Chopin—where the composer, sculpted in mid-action at his piano, continues hammering out some mazurka or other while the inevitable young woman seated beneath the instrument, her hair covered with a veil and her feet curiously huge, apparently quite enthralled, covers her eyes with one hand while in the grip of ecstasy—God, that's beautiful!—or exasperation—God, get me away from this creep!

Number 4 Rue Murillo is in fact quite a handsome building, but Bernie's lodgings consisted of three maids' quarters merged into one, overlooking the courtyard. Bernie ushered Max into the main area, which combined the functions of living room, kitchen, and dining room, and which also contained his bed. Through an open door, Max noticed some very state-of-the-art computer equipment in the room of the very intelligent stepson, who seemed to be absent. Bernie, as agreed, served Max a beer, into which, to his great consternation, the other emptied half the alcohol exhibited in the park. Then the little man attempted as usual to distract the pianist, to make him forget the approaching moment of the concert, seeking out arguments and ideas with all the more difficulty in that Max's intoxication worsened with each passing minute—although, to look on the bright side, it seemed to have dampened his stage fright.

At around seven-thirty, holding each other up as best they could, they slowly made their way down Avenue de Messine towards Salle Gaveau. And at eight o'clock sharp, after a fair number of efforts to keep Max on his feet, Bernie propelled him towards the piano using his habitual technique. What was not predictable was that the other man walked with a firm step towards the instrument, even though, in his vision clouded by imbibition, the keyboard was no longer its usual single maxillary but an authentic pair of jaws that this time was preparing, as sure as anything, to draw him in, chew him up, and spit him out. Now, as the entire room stood up to applaud him the moment he appeared on-stage, in an interminable Niagara of acclaim that was even livelier than last week, and as the ovation grew only more enthusiastic with no signs of abating, Max, who was no longer in full possession of his faculties, deduced that the concert was over. He therefore bowed deeply to the public several times and headed with a no less resolute step back towards the wings, under the horrified eyes of Parisy—but, without a second's hesitation, Bernie gripped Max by the shoulders, spun him around, and, with a hearty shove, vigorously sent him back on-stage and so off you go: sonata.

"Well done, Bernard," said Parisy. "That was good. That was really good."

"It's not always easy, you know," Bernie pointed out. "It can be quite a physical job, at times."

SEVEN

TWO HOURS LATER, sobered up by the trial of the concert, nerves at rest but mind at zero, Max Delmarc was dozing on the back seat of a taxi. When it then came to a halt, Max, opening his eyes, recognised his building before noticing, in front of the door, a very large and immobile dog staring fixedly in his direction. Once the driver was paid, the dog continued to stare at Max as he got out of the cab: it was a truly voluminous beast, of Newfoundland or mastiff proportions, apparently peaceful and friendly, which then left, pulled by a long leash whose taut line Max's eyes followed in a tracking shot to arrive at a person of the female sex, viewed from behind. Now even from behind, even from afar, even under street lamps fifty percent of which were burnt out, Max had no trouble recognising the extraordinarily beautiful woman whom he occasionally ran into in the neighbourhood. Here she was now, walking away, followed by her animal, towards Square de la Villette, and at this time of night.

Max is really not the sort to accost strange women in the street, especially at this time of night. It's a matter of principle, of course, but not entirely: even if he wanted to, he would be incapable. Still, maybe as a delayed effect of all the alcohol consumed that day—no doubt, but perhaps not only—he was now starting to follow this woman with the firm intention of speaking to her. He had no idea what he would say, didn't really care, and wasn't even surprised that he didn't care—he'd find something at the last minute. Alas, coming up behind her, he was suddenly surprised to hear her talking to herself, until he noticed that she was conversing with a mobile phone. No chance of accosting her under these conditions, so he passed her with a quick step as if he had other intentions, without turning around or even knowing where he was going, forced to look like he was heading somewhere, improvising a target that would in fact be Square de la Villette three blocks away. Not many people at this hour in the small streets of the neighbourhood: the noise of his footsteps echoed too loudly, seemed to ricochet against the dark façades and, as it made his gait awkward, Max uneasily imagined himself seen from behind. Then, arriving at the square, he formulated a very simple plan: he would double back to cross paths with the woman and this time he'd speak to her. He still had no idea what he might say, but this, oddly enough, struck him as negligible.

Having reached the square, then, he retraced his steps and spotted her from a distance coming towards him, the dog walking in front of its mistress in hazy silhouette. As this silhouette became more precise, making it clear to Max that she was still talking into her little phone, he could only abstain once more from accosting her. Head lowered, staring at the tips of his shoes, he passed by her as quickly as possible and dashed off to take refuge at home—she must have noticed my little act, at worst I must look like a nutter, at best like an idiot, and in any case it's a disaster. He pushed open the main door of his building, registering that the lights were still on in Alice's rooms but not slowing his pace. Then, entering his studio, he tossed his raincoat carelessly on the divan, not lingering awhile as he usually did but heading directly into his bedroom, where he threw off his clothes in a rage and went to bed in a rage. But after a moment of immobility, he was hurriedly throwing them back on again, perhaps inside-out, recrossing the studio, and walking hastily out. She must be home by now, but you never know, still no idea what I might say but basically what do I have to lose? But wait, what do I see: there she is. She's there, the dog is there, they're there.

Max approached, determined. The dog again began staring at Max benignly, without emitting any growls or showing the slightest glimpse of fang, seeming as gentle as he was huge—can somebody please tell me what dogs like that are good for? She too watched Max approach, showing no surprise at all, and without the slightest trace of a frown or self-protective spray made from natural pepper extracts.

"Don't be afraid," Max stammered a little too fast, "I'll just take a second. The thing is, I've been seeing you around for a long time."

"That's true," she smiled. That's good, Max said to himself, she's noticed me, that's already something.

"And so," said Max, "the thing is, I just wanted to know who you are." Cheeky fellow.

"Well," she smiled, "I live at number 55, and as you see I'm walking my dog" (I'm at number 59, myself, Max calculated). "Normally it's my children" (ouch! Max said to himself) "who walk him, but tonight they're out." Silence and another smile. It was high time to wrap this up if he didn't want to look like a . . . Max, who emphatically did not want to look like a . . . , bowed slightly, smiling in turn as broadly as he could. "Well, then," he said, "I bid you an excellent night."

Crossing through the courtyard once more, Max again saw the light in Alice's window but he refrained from going in to say goodnight. And yet he often went to see her after a concert, to tell her how it had gone, how was your day, that kind of thing, but tonight, no, not possible. He wouldn't have been able to prevent himself telling her what had just happened. He had already made enough of an ass of himself as it was, and besides he was too agitated. So he paced for a while around his studio, naturally poured himself one last drink, lifted the fall board on his piano only to close it again, leafed through a newspaper without reading it, and ended up putting himself to bed: long thought for the woman with the dog, barely a tiny thought for Rose, my sleeping pill, and goodnight.

EIGHT

OVER THE FOLLOWING DAYS, Max met the woman with the dog at an unusual rhythm, much more sustained than over all the past years. After their brief encounter a few nights before, they now had to greet each other, and even smile at each other since their rapid exchange had transpired in perfect civility. These smiles, however, proved to be of variable amplitudes and models. One evening when he saw her looking more elegant than usual (to be that elegant, she must have been going to some social event, and who knows with whom—you might even wonder if Max was starting to get a bit jealous, things can move so fast in this kind of situation), she gave him an amused smile, almost collusive, or merely indulgent, that seemed to prolong itself even after she had turned her back on him—which had the effect of making Max feel ridiculous, then flattered, then ridiculous at feeling flattered.

Another time, late in the morning, he observed her coming from the other end of the street, dressed in a jogging suit—a jogging suit from Hermès, of course, but a jogging suit all the same—and dragging a shopping trolley behind her—shopping trolley from Conran, granted, but a shopping trolley nonetheless. That morning she was less made-up than usual, her hair less managed, less victorious and arched; she must simply have been coming back from doing the shopping and not have appreciated overmuch being spotted like this, because her smile, this time minuscule, struck Max as noticeably cooler. On yet another day, he saw her in front of number 55 trying to park her car in the rain—a small black Audi, Max noted—in a space that was somewhat tight for the vehicle's dimensions. Twisted all the way around in her seat toward the Audi's rear window, apparently absorbed by her task, she flashed Max a smile that this time had a more complicit nuance, given the difficulty of the undertaking— one of those smiles that make you gently raise your eyes heavenward, that take you aside as witness to life's little challenges, especially since on top of it all it's raining and since this movement of the lips is further softened by the mist and mobile reflections of the streaming windows. Max, who didn't own a car, who hadn't known until then that this woman had one, immediately committed her number plate to memory. In each of these instances the dog was nowhere to be seen and, on each of these occasions, Max made a point of showing himself as discreet as possible, responding to those smiles with a courteous reserve, or a half-tone just below, in short behaving like a perfect gentleman. Still not wanting to risk looking like a . . .

The day of that complicit smile, Max was expecting a visit from Parisy. It was the first time the impresario came to his home, anxious to verify the performer's good spirits before the taping of a televised concert. Prestigious orchestra, exceptional soloists, live broadcast conditions in a studio at Radio-France, and audience by invitation only, but the show would be pre-recorded, then screened late in the evening on the cultural channel. Although Parisy, dressed that day in a dark suit meant to absorb and conceal sweat, came on the pretext of having a last look at the scores, of fine-tuning a few technical details, he mainly wanted to reassure himself that Max, nervous as always during the past few days at the prospect, was not going to misbehave beyond reason while awaiting the concert hour. Normally the impresario delegated this surveillance work, but this time the stakes were too high to be supervised by Bernie alone. Max nonetheless seemed rather distracted, mixing up the figures embossed on the Audi's number plate and the bars on his score.

"Aren't you thirsty?" said Max. "Don't you want something to drink?"

"Listen," Parisy began, "let me just say straight away that I'd rather you—"

"Never fear," Max interrupted, "no alcohol today, don't worry. I'm not even sure what's the matter with me, to tell you the truth. I don't even feel like any. Coffee?"

"Gladly," said the other.

Via the intercom, Max asked Alice to make some coffee,

inviting her to join them. Then, closing the score, he dropped on to the divan with a yawn.

"Everything O.K.?" worried Parisy. "Not too nervous?"

"Oddly enough, no," said Max. "TV doesn't affect me the way concert halls do."

"And anyway, it's not live," Parisy reminded him. "You have nothing to worry about. If need be, they can always retake a passage if something goes wrong."

"Yeah, yeah," said Max, standing up to go and cast a few sullen glances out of the studio window. Under the combined effects of the rain and wind, there was nothing and nobody to see in the street, except that they were still offering the usual twenty-five percent off the linoleum rolls lined up on the pavement, the green neon of the pharmacy cross was blinking as always, and at the second-hand clothes shop next door everything was still ten francs an item. Whereupon Alice appeared, carrying a tray.

Nearly as tall, even thinner, and two years younger than Max, hair as white as his, slightly awkward, barely made-up, adorned only with a thin gold chain around her neck, Alice was wearing a very lightweight, light-coloured grey ensemble, very loose-fitting and very neutralising. Having set the tray on a chair near the divan, she walked smiling up to Parisy, who rose sharply from his seat to bow stiffly before straightening up again. Looking at her gravely, he seemed impressed to the point of starting to stutter and sweating outrageously the moment she addressed him. Max looked on in surprise at his manager, not used to seeing Alice produce such an effect on a man, but amused to see this one so off-balance. Parisy, so as to regain his bearing, forced himself to make a little joke, and Alice immediately burst out laughing. As with some not-very-pretty women, it didn't take much to provoke her hilarity, and so she laughed a bit too often even though her laughter sounded raucous, like a cry of rage or suffering, as if laughing were painful, as if she were trying to expectorate something with great difficulty.

Parisy, however, did not seem to be shocked by this laugh as much as was Max, who normally had such a hard time coping with it that he carefully refrained from saying anything even remotely funny in her presence—except that something that wasn't funny at all could still make her burst out laughing, provoking a chain effect of further laughter, in ricochet, increasingly inextinguishable and frenetic the more one tried, more and more sternly, to check the process. Max, in any case, decided to clarify the situation.

"Well then," he said, "let me introduce my sister. I don't believe you two know each other."

NINE

YOU, ON THE OTHER HAND, I know perfectly well; I know exactly what you're thinking. You were imagining that Max was yet another ladies' man, one of those classic schemers, charming and all that, but a touch tiresome. First Alice, then Rose, and now the woman with the dog: these episodes led you to assume the profile of a man drowning in amorous intrigues. You found this profile rather conventional, and you wouldn't be wrong. But that's not it at all. The proof is that, of the three women who up until now have figured in the life of this artist, one is his sister, the other a memory, the third an apparition, and that's it. There aren't any others, you were wrong to worry; so let's get back to it.

They'd had their coffee, during which time Parisy hadn't taken his eyes off Alice until she'd left the room. Then he'd pointed out that it was getting late and it was time to get a move on and that his car was parked on Rue de Clignancourt, so Max went off to don his pianist's uniform. And there again, even though he proceeded without nervousness, and even with unusual calm, two more buttons chose to desert his garment, one rolling off to hide under a chest of drawers, the other going underground in a crack in the floor. It must have been a season in the life cycle of Max's outfits, some autumn of his wardrobe. But for the moment, they were too rushed to indulge in long searches. Alice, summoned back, indicated she wouldn't have time to intervene, and Max had to swap his dress shirt for a more ordinary model. It was annoying but he'd make do, and they left in haste in Parisy's Volvo towards the sixteenth *arrondissement*, which if you leave from Château-Rouge is almost at the opposite end of Paris, the intramural equivalent of New Zealand.

"Rotten weather," muttered Parisy. "We'll try to avoid the centre of town."

The rain, in fact, having continued to fall, certainly would not fail to produce its usual coagulation of obstructions. To avoid losing time by crossing through a congested Paris, they agreed to take the outer roads. They first followed rectilinear Rue de Clignancourt, then took a right on to Rue Championnet to get to Rue des Poissonniers, before reaching the outer boulevards named after marshals, whose pavements were sporadically populated with very young women of Nigerian, Lithuanian, Ghanaian, Moldavian, Senegalese, Slovakian, Albanian, or Ivorian nationality. Skimpily clad beneath their umbrellas, they were more or less constantly observed by four categories of men: first the Bulgarian or Turkish procurers scattered about the vicinity, snug and warm in their high-octane sedans, having made the standard recommendations (At least thirty tricks a day; fewer than twenty-five and we break your leg); secondly the customers for whose benefit, day and night, they declaimed in every tone the same perfect alexandrine, classically balanced with caesura at the hemistich (It's fifteen for a blow and thirty for the works); thirdly the forces of law and order that, for their part, emerged especially at night, though not too aggressively (Hello hello, it's the police, do you have ID papers? Nothing? You sure? Not even a photocopy?); not to mention, fourthly, the television crews making sure that, when the nth report on the subject was broadcast after prime time, in accordance with the law on the protection of privacy, the faces of these working girls appeared duly pixelated on the screen. These young women, these young girls, who often were not even eighteen, began to thin out after Boulevard Suchet, then were completely gone by Rue de Boulainvilliers, along which Parisy's car glided up to the Maison de la Radio.

Recording was supposed to start at six, but they'd need a little time to get used to the studio, negotiate with the lighting technicians and sound engineers, and go over two or three details with the orchestra one last time, even though everything had been settled after several weeks of rehearsals. Then they'd move on to make-up, filing before the mirrors in groups of three, in the hands of specialists who were often quite pretty and who handled matters with attentive indifference. In any case, they were only putting make-up on the soloists and the conductor; the bulk of the troupe would remain in its natural state, with just a little touch of powder for the melancholics and the sanguines. Although only a minimal space was needed to contain the orchestra, the studio was still much more cramped than it would appear on-screen, but it's always the same story with television: space, screen, ideas, projects, everything is smaller there than in the normal world.

After disembodied voices had given the countdown, the concert could begin. The conductor was fairly exasperating, full of mannered grimaces, unctuous and enveloping motions, coded little signs addressed to different categories of performers, fingers on his lips and inopportune thrusts of his hips. Following his lead, the instrumentalists themselves began to act like smart alecks: taking advantage of a frill in the score that allowed him to shine a little, to stand out from the masses for the space of a few bars, an oboist demonstrated extreme concentration, even over-playing it to win the right to a close-up. Thanks to several high-lighted phrases allocated to them, two English horns also did their little number a moment later. And Max, who had very quickly lost the scrap of stage fright that had come over him that day and was even starting to feel bored, himself began to make pianist faces in turn, looking preoccupied, pulling his head deep into his shoulders or excessively arching his back, depending on the tempo; smiling at the instrument, the work, the very essence of music, himself—you have to keep interested somehow.

Then, once it was all wrapped up, it was time to go home.

Taking advantage of the fact that for once he might look good, Max opted not to have his make-up removed. When Parisy apologised for not being able to drive him back, he set off on foot. The rain had abated and he crossed the Seine over the Pont de Grenelle up to the Allée des Cygnes, a fragment of the river's spine lined with benches and trees that he followed up to the Pont de Bir-Hakeim, via which he reached the Passy *métro*. His plan was to take Line 6 of the urban network, change at Place de l'Étoile, and, from there, head back to Barbès. The elevated Passy stop is very pretty, very airy and chic, overhung by tall buildings as distinguished as flagships, so handsome that they look unoccupied and strictly decorative. Max waited calmly for the train to appear.

Once it arrived, as it was emptying itself and being filled by several passengers, another train pulled in from the opposite direction, heading towards Place de la Nation; it stopped, emptied out and filled up like the others. And once Max was aboard, standing against a windowed door, who did he see, or at least think he saw in the facing train at just the same level as his, which was about to leave? Rose, of course.

Rose, dressed in a dark grey suit beneath a pale-beige, much-pleated raincoat, apparently lightweight, cut from what must be called soft poplin and belted at the waist. The garment wasn't familiar to Max, naturally, but that aside, she didn't seem to have changed much in thirty years.

TEN

EMERGENCY. Although the warning signal had just sounded, Max rushed perilously out of the carriage: he jumped off in profile, Egyptian-style, to avoid the doors that briefly slammed into his shoulders and had closed before he landed on the platform. From there, he tried again to make out Rose through the superimposed windows of the two trains, one of which, his, was now rolling towards Étoile. It left the other one more visible for an instant, before the latter started off towards Nation two seconds later, and without Max being able to verify that it did in fact contain Rose. He wasn't completely certain it was her but, for the space of an instant, the resemblance had struck him as indisputable; a resemblance wearing a raincoat in which Max, while he had never seen it before, recognised what he believed he'd surmised of Rose's sartorial tastes, thirty years earlier.

Nothing is certain, but you never know. Max started to run down the platform towards the long transfer corridors, bounding up the stairways four steps at a time to reach the opposite platform, where he waited for the arrival of the next train. Which took a ridiculous amount of time. The whole enterprise was absurd. You don't follow a tube train. But then again, why not? While waiting, to make time go faster, he feverishly reread the *métro* regulations—making sure that the five categories of passengers who ride for free still included, albeit in last place, unaccompanied persons who have lost both hands. The train arrived, Max got on. Although this train abounded in unoccupied seats, Max remained standing, posting himself next to a door through the window of which he could inspect the platforms of the stations to come. Once they had left Passy via the Bir-Hakeim bridge, he had another opportunity to examine the Seine, after which, between the ensuing stations, he could once more ponder the city.

It's just that the Étoile–Nation line, which provides the link between the affluent and working-class neighbourhoods— although these adjectives, melding together to the point of leapfrogging over each other, of taking themselves for each other, are no longer what they used to be—runs above ground for the most part, enjoying as no other line the light of day, from which nearly one station in two benefits. It constantly emerges from the earth only to plunge back down again in a sinusoid, sea serpent or roller coaster, ghost train or coitus.

But already, the platform of Bir-Hakeim station, first stop after fording the river, bore no trace of the raincoat. Nor was there any glimpse of beige at Dupleix, a clear and well-lit station beneath a sky of double-sloping glass; and as they began to pick up speed beside the buildings, eye-level with kitchens and bathrooms, living rooms and bedrooms and hotel rooms, and as dusk began to fall and electric lights threatened to go on, Max began to see his enterprise as highly dubious. Although the building windows were most often masked by curtains, nets, or blinds, he caught fugitive glimpses of the scenes in the flats. Three men sitting around a table. A child illuminated by a desk lamp. A woman passing from one room to another. A cat, or maybe a dog, lying on a cushion. After not finding the slightest trace of Rose at La Motte-Picquet-Grenelle, Max's doubts about the viability of his project deepened further. He was almost at the point of giving up, but no, he persevered. Better that than doing nothing.

After a while, he accorded no more than a summary glance to the station platforms parading by. Instead, he inventoried what came between them, the individuals and objects decorating the balconies and terraces that he saw from the rushing train at a downward angle—laundry stretched on a line or a clothes horse, mopeds leaning against a lowered shutter, shopping trolleys, push-chairs, and broken down washing machines, soaked cardboard boxes, garden chairs, rugs, ladders, footstools, plants and flower boxes in which geraniums claimed the lion's share, old broken toys, plastic basins, washbowls, and pails with mop handles thrusting out at an angle. Not to mention, months after New Year's Day, the old Christmas trees of which only a rusty spine remained, nor the parabolic antennae all facing in the same direction like vertical fields of sunflowers, nor the idle women in various states of dress, leaning on their elbows against railings and watching the elevated *métro* pass by, full of single men like Max, who stared back at them.

After Pasteur station, Max, who had lost all hope of finding Rose and ended up taking a folding seat, cast only an absent eye towards the platforms. As long as the *métro* remained elevated, he observed the landscape and, when it plunged underground, he pondered the two men on the seats opposite his, but in that regard there was nothing very attractive to see: one, with a suitcase at his feet, offered a view of the cut on his scalp; the other, with an expressionless face, was consulting a brochure entitled *How to Recover Your Alimony Payments*. Max opted to study his *métro* ticket.

As nothing special is happening in this scene, we might as well take the time to look more closely at this ticket. There's actually a lot that can be said about these tickets, about their secondary uses—toothpick, fingernail scraper, or paper cutter, guitar pick or plectrum, bookmark, crumb sweeper, conduit or straw for controlled substances, awning for a doll's house, micro-notebook, souvenir, or support for a phone number that you scribble for a girl in case of emergency—and their various fates—folded lengthwise in halves or quarters and liable to be slid under an engagement ring, signet ring, or wristwatch; folded in six or even eight in accordion fashion, ripped into confetti, peeled in a spiral like an apple, then tossed into the wastepaper-baskets of the *métro* system, on the floor of the system, between the tracks of the system, or even cast out of the system, in the gutter, the street, at home to play heads or tails: heads magnetic stripe, tails printed side—but perhaps this isn't the moment to go into all of that.

When the *métro* re-emerged from under the ground, Max might also have absorbed himself in the viaducts they were rumbling over, good old handsome viaducts, good solid iron architecture, intelligent and dignified, but no: as his plan of pursuit came undone before his eyes, soon wilted like a poppy, here he was getting off the train at Nationale station. Then, as he had nothing left to do, he began to walk, without imagination, still following Line 6, but in the open air, crossing the savage, cursory, and poorly laid-out space that runs beneath those viaducts like a path. This space sometimes contains various pedlar's carts, flea markets, stalls, or impromptu basketball courts, but it's mainly a place for the relatively anarchic parking of cars: a cold narrow corridor, a no-man's-land beneath the prickly metal noise of the convoys, where no-one ever ventures without a vague sense of disquiet. And so Max walked, following this route up to the Seine, which he crossed in the opposite direction from before, then continuing up to Bel-Air where, exhausted, he waited for the next train.

ELEVEN

BEL-AIR is an elevated station isolated between two tunnels, an island that hangs over the depopulated Rue du Sahel like an oasis. Supported by two rows of five columns, awnings of painted wood shelter the platforms, extended by glass canopies. These platforms appear shorter than in other stations, and overall Bel-Air gives off an aura of humility. It calls to mind a small village station, poor cousin or disowned sister of George V.

We would have no reason to linger on this station, except that it was here, against all likelihood, that Max believed he again recognised Rose. This is how it happened: Max arrived on the empty platform, Nation-bound side, when a train pulled in from the opposite direction, towards Étoile—this train business never ends. Passengers got off, almost none got on, then the train set off. Max distractedly glanced at the travellers as they made their way towards the platform exit before disappearing into the stairway. Now among them, from the rear, in three-quarter view, it indeed appeared to be her again, apart from the fact that this time she was wearing navy-blue slacks and an apple-green zipped-up jacket, or something like that, he didn't really have time to look, all of this transpired in a mere couple of seconds. Still, Max did not take the time to reason it out, to deem it odd that Rose should be getting off a train in that direction whereas he, less than an hour earlier, had begun tailing her in the opposite direction—not to mention that she wasn't even dressed the same. Neither space nor time nor clothing matched, but never mind, let's go. Run for it.

He began running under the twenty-four pairs of uncovered neon lights that reached to just above his skull. He ran skirting the classic attributes of a *métro* platform, monitor screens, fire extinguishers, plastic chairs, mirrors, pictograms warning against the dangers of electrocution, and rubbish bins—four rubbish bins on the side going to Étoile while only two on the Nation side, why is that? Does one have less to throw away when coming from the rich neighbourhoods? Max did not have time to deal with this question right now, but even so, as he rushed back out of the station, the idea flashed through his mind that he'd just used up a ticket for nothing.

When he found himself back on Rue du Sahel, once again there was nothing to be seen, neither to the left nor to the right. He decided to take a footbridge at the edge of the station, straddling the tracks and protected by a fence against which rested empty and more or less battered cartons (Orangina, Coke,

Yoplait), six pebbles, a litre bottle with star-shaped cracks, an un-usable pair of Air Force-blue espadrilles, a little green plastic sand shovel without its pail, all surrounded by a palpable silence, the famous silence of the twelfth *arrondissement*.

And in the midst of this silence, nothing and no-one as far as the eye could see. Right. Let's analyse the situation. It's one of four things. Either it was Rose at Passy in a beige raincoat. Or it was Rose at Bel-Air in a green jacket. Or it was Rose in both in-stances, having changed clothes in less than an hour to take the *métro* twice in opposite directions, which wasn't very likely. Or it was she in neither instance, which was all too likely. Go back home. Take the *métro* again, plunge back underground. That's right, buy another ticket. And stop making that face.

And for the entire duration of this long return, fourteen stops and two transfers, the *métro* seemed to him dirtier and more de-pressing than ever, despite the zeal of the cleaning services. We all know that in the beginning (historical factoid) the immaculate tiling of the subway system, modelled on that of clinics, was in-tended to lessen or even eliminate worrisome ideas injected by the subterranean depths—darkness, dampness, miasmas, humid-ity, illness, epidemic, collapse, rats—by disguising this burrow as an impeccable cloakroom. Except that they ended up with exactly the opposite result. For there exists a malediction of cloakrooms. Even a slightly dirty cloakroom always looks dirtier than a much dirtier non-cloakroom. It's just that on any white expanse, be it ice floe or bed sheet, it takes almost nothing, the tiniest suspect detail, for everything to turn, just as it only takes one fly for the entire sugar bowl to go into mourning. Nothing is sadder than a stain between two white tiles, like dirt under a fingernail or tartar on a tooth. Once back home, Max didn't even feel like taking a shower.

But the next morning, as he emerged from his building, he again ran into the woman with the dog. This time she was displaying her customary elegance—neighbourhood elegance, halfway between that of her supposed evenings out and the outfit in which she did her shopping—and no sooner had he spied her than she walked straight up to him.

"Good morning," she immediately said. "I saw you last night on television, by chance, as I was channel-surfing." She paused for a moment to smile, as if in apology for this verb. "Ah," she resumed, "I didn't realise we had a famous musician in the neighbourhood. I'm going to tell my husband" (ouch! Max said to himself again) "to buy your recordings." She smiled at him again, differently this time from all the other times, before walking off on her very narrow high heels, and Max, turning back protractedly to watch her move away, thought that you can say what you will, but music has its advantages.

TWELVE

SEVERAL DAYS LATER, Max had to attend a benefit for he wasn't sure what, but something that Parisy deemed couldn't hurt in terms of public image. A succession of musicians were to follow one another on stage for brief performances; Max knew most of them, almost all friends, relaxed atmosphere, zero stage fright. The atmosphere in the hall was also much more relaxed than usual for a concert: families paying very little attention, huge number of children, not exactly the typical audience profile for classical music. When the time came for Max, who was in fact due to play Schumann's *Scenes from Childhood*, he sat at the piano amid an astounding hubbub: from the seats came a cacophony of calls, chatting, laughter, and crinkled wrappings that he had never experienced while playing—for, despite what they say, the public for classical music is fairly well behaved; even when it disapproves, it generally keeps quiet.

Without letting the noise deter him, Max thus attacked

"From Foreign Lands and Peoples" in an environment so festive that he could barely hear the opening bars. Still, as he continued to play, he felt the noise begin to dissolve like a cloud, open on to a silent blue sky; he noticed that he was circumventing the audience, drawing it to him like a bull, focusing it, holding it, pulling it taut. Soon the silence in the room was as loud, magnetic and nervous as the music itself; these two fluxes bounced back and forth and vibrated in harmony—without Max mastering in the slightest what his ten fingers were doing on the keyboard, without him knowing where this was coming from, from his work or his experience or from some other place, like lightning, like a great unexpected ray of light. The phenomenon is rare, but it can happen, and twenty minutes later, no sooner had he finished "The Poet Speaks" than, after a pause, an instant of suspended amazement, an ovation burst out that Max wouldn't have swapped for a triumph at the Théâtre des Champs-Elysées.

Champagne. It was the least he could do, he had to recover a bit. Champagne, of course, but soon the programme organisers came up, asking Max to sign a few CDs by popular demand. Of course, said Max, just one more little glass and I'm all yours. He went back into the room where they had set up a small table for him, behind which was a chair, and in front of which a rather considerable queue had indeed begun forming. Very quickly, the *Scenes from Childhood* that Max had recorded two years earlier would be out of stock, then almost as quickly Schumann in general, then any other Romantic music they had available. These went to a long queue of intimidated men with smug smiles, excited women with ready smiles, and even very well-groomed children with serious smiles, and Max signed, signed, signed, ah, all the times in one's life that one has to write one's name.

After a while, the turn came for a man of rather handsome appearance, with an open face and well-cut suit, who deposited three CDs in front of Max while leaning towards him. "You don't know me," he said, without a smile, "but you know my wife and my dog."

Max, immediately understanding what was what, thought his hour had come. We ourselves, knowing that his death is nigh, might have reason to believe that his passing was imminent, but no, nothing of the sort—we could even say things went quite well. The man's spouse must have told him about their rapid nocturnal encounter, apparently without this triggering any reaction of jealousy or homicidal vengeance. The man himself, he explained, practised a profession that was not unrelated to the artistic sphere.

"What name should I make them out to?" Max asked hopefully.

"They're for me," the man said. "My name is Georges and I came alone, without my wife and children." It would not be that day that Max learned the name of the woman with the dog.

Everything went quite well, then, but Max was still a little nervous when leaving the site of the benefit concert. While he hadn't, for lack of stage fright, felt the need to drink before playing, he had on the other hand downed a good amount of champagne afterwards with his colleagues, in decreasing numbers until none remained and he had to leave in turn. Then he passed alone through several bars that he also successively closed down, after which, my word, it was indeed time to go home to bed.

It is late, it is cold, it is drizzling or dribbling, it's still with a fairly steady gait that Max advances in his empty street at this hour of the night. Then, as he approaches number 55 en route to his building, he casts a semi-circular glance ahead to verify that the husband of the woman with the dog isn't lurking in a recess, having reconsidered and lain in wait for Max's return with evil on his mind. No, no-one. But would that Max had cast that glance behind instead, for suddenly he feels himself grabbed by the collar of his coat, thrown down on to the pavement, and now he's lying stretched out on his back with two fellows on top of him, masked by scarves—but, scarves or no, Max has thrown his forearm over his face in protection—who undertake a systematic rifling of his person. To do this, they tear open his raincoat violently, with so little care that two or three new buttons jump off and roll together towards the gutter—no doubt about it, it's plain to see, this really is the season of buttons.

The men methodically extract everything they find in Max's pockets and, after a moment, as the latter reckons that this is all beginning to drag on, it occurs to him to cry out, oh, not cry out for real, cry out just a little bit, you know, for form's sake, in case it could summon someone. But first, he manages to emit only a feeble and timid whine, like a slightly peevish whimper, and second, he feels a hand clamp on to his mouth to shut him up. He could, of course, push that hand aside to keep shouting; it's only a small hand of adolescent size. But he's afraid that another hand, not necessarily larger but holding a weapon, might administer a more radical treatment, and more to the point, he notices the briny, grimy taste of that hand on his lips, which he prefers to shut tight out of hygienic reflex.

And besides, truth to tell, he decides it's better just to lie back, to simply let himself go, let things take their course. He is suddenly enveloped by an almost comfortable, almost shamefully voluptuous resignation, in the renunciation of all and the vanity of everything. It works the same as when you decide, screwed if you do and screwed if you don't, to give yourself over to the anaesthetist, who fixes a mask over your face in the perfect scialytic light and ideal calm of the operating theatre, under the eyes of skull-capped surgeons. And correlatively, even though this entire process unfolds at top speed, time seems to Max to distend and multiply, as if all this were happening in slow motion despite the nervous fever of the two fellows installed on top of him.

He knows he shouldn't do it, but sometimes one has troublesome reflexes: Max stops protecting his eyes to see who these guys are—they're obviously very young, but what do they look like?

But their faces are hidden by scarves, and Max, seized by a jolt of exasperation and before he realises what he's doing, rips one of them off. He uncovers a rather indistinct, and indeed very young, face, on which he barely has time to glimpse an expression that quickly veers from bewildered to furious, indignant to vengeful, then the time to notice a foreshortened arm raised above him, prolonged by a stiletto that the unmasked young man, surely no less horrified than Max, drives deep into his throat, just above the Adam's apple. The stiletto first pierces Max's skin, before its momentum carries it through his tracheal artery and oesophagus, damaging large vessels of the carotid and jugular type, after which, gliding between two vertebrae—seventh cervical and first dorsal—it severs Max's spinal cord, and there is no-one left on the scene.

Everything is dark in the surrounding buildings; all the windows are black; no-one is looking at anything except the dog of the woman with the dog, still awake at this hour on the fourth floor of number 55. He's a sweet and meditative dog, as Max had immediately noticed, a good pensive dog who, suffering from bouts of insomnia, sometimes stares out the window at night to pass the time, and who has just witnessed this regrettable incident. If the beast's dreamy nature predisposes him towards visions, perhaps it will now see, as a little encore, Max's soul rising gently into the welcoming ether.

II

THIRTEEN

NO.

No, no ascension, no ether, no big to-do. And yet it seemed
that even after he was dead, Max continued to experience things.
He found himself naked in a single bed that occupied about a
quarter of a small, dark room whose walls, painted ochre with
patina effects, absorbed the light of a weak bedside lamp standing on a bedside table, the dimness increased by a fringed maroon
cloth spread over the beige lampshade. Once he had opened his
eyes, and after several minutes spent looking around without seeing much of anything, Max pulled away the cloth without this
revealing a great deal more of his new environment. A few more
minutes passed, during which he mustered feeble efforts to understand what could possibly have happened, but in vain. Giving up, he finally got out of bed, fighting off a brief dizzy spell
before gathering up his trousers, which he found carefully folded
over the back of a chair. He pulled them on, then set off towards

the door that he assumed, for no particular reason, would be locked.

It wasn't. But although this door opened without difficulty, it led only to a long, empty corridor, punctuated by other closed doors between which, at regular intervals, wall-lamps gave off the faint halos of night-lights. The corridor was so long that you couldn't see either end of it; so empty that it was nothing, revealed nothing, provided no more information than if the door had in fact been bolted. Max, bare-chested, was about to close his door again when he noticed, far down the corridor to the left, an indistinct figure wearing a yellow dressing gown who detached himself tentatively from the wall, evidently venturing out like Max. Max was hesitating about which course to take, whether to wave or hide, uncertain as to the nature of this figure, when he saw it jump back at the arrival of another silhouette.

White in colour and emerging from who knows where, this second figure seemed gently but firmly to admonish Yellow Dressing Gown, who immediately vanished. Apparently White Silhouette then noticed Max, who watched it walk towards him, become transformed in its approach into a young woman who was the spitting image of Peggy Lee—tall, nurse's blouse, very light hair pulled back and held with a hair-slide. With the same implacable softness, she enjoined Max to go back into his room.

"You have to stay in here," she said—moreover, in Peggy Lee's voice. "Someone will be along to see you soon."

"But," started Max, getting no further, as the young woman

immediately negated this incipient objection with a gentle rustling of her fingers, deployed like a flight of birds in the air between them. When you got down to it, she did look phenomenally like Peggy Lee, the same kind of big, milk-fed blonde, with a fleshy, dimpled face, full figure and broad forehead, invasive cheeks, wide mouth, and excessive lower lip forming the permanent smile of a zealous cub mistress. More reassuring than arousing, she exuded complete wholesomeness and strict morals.

Back in his room, Max examined things more closely. There wasn't enough space for much furniture other than his bed and the bedside table, both made of mahogany; a minuscule cupboard, perhaps made of oak and containing a few spare clothes in Max's size; an elegant little table roughly the size of a sideboard; the chair on which his trousers had been folded, and that was it. No decoration on the walls, no knick-knacks, no magazines, not a book in sight, no Gideon Bible in the bedside drawer or tourist brochure that might indicate where he was, what he could do there, what there was to see in the area, with all the usual timetables and price lists. In sum, a sober, comfortable room, the kind probably found in certain abbeys that have been refitted as spiritual retreats, intended for souls who dispose of equally comfortable incomes. An air-conditioned space, perfectly quiet owing to the fact that, alas, there were no windows, and still more so because it contained neither radio nor television. A door made of some translucent material led to a decently designed bathroom, even though there was no mirror above the sink. As Max tried to see his reflection in this translucent material, he vaguely made out a dark patch at the base of his neck. But something made him hesitate before bringing his hand to it, and in any case, at that same moment, the door to his room unexpectedly opened to reveal a visitor.

The visitor was perhaps a bit taller than Max, clearly a bit thinner, well built and of elegant bearing—things that Max would ordinarily find rather irksome. The man displayed a casualness bordering on insolence, reminiscent of a fair number of clowns that Max had known in his professional life: art directors or publicity heads of record companies, critics or producers of specialised festivals in some narrowly defined sub-category of Baroque. His light, loose-fitting clothes also fitted him a bit too well, beige linen suit over an anthracite T-shirt and docksiders. He seemed excessively aware of his appearance; his hair denoted just the right amount of negligence, thick and brushed back with one discreetly rebellious strand falling forward. With his manicured nails, weekly ultraviolet treatments, and exfoliated skin, he radiated gym clubs, hair salons and beauty salons, fitting rooms and tea rooms. "Hello, Max," he uttered without warmth, "pleased to meet you. My name is Christian Béliard, but you may call me Christian. I'll be looking after you."

All of this—and those who know anything about Max can see it coming—does not augur well. Max does not particularly like it when a stranger calls him by his first name straight away, like an American; he does not appreciate very much that this stranger is addressing him in a nonchalant tone and hardly looking at him; and he especially does not care for the relaxed, professionally indifferent attitude displayed by this stranger who, while talking to him, is casting distracted glances around the room as if conducting an inspection. On top of which, Max really doesn't see why this chump, for whom he feels an immediate dislike, claims to be looking after him, or who the hell he thinks he is. He would prefer that someone first explain to him, politely, what he's done to deserve all this distant solicitude, and what they, in fact, are actually doing here, and particularly what he, Max, is doing here at all. But, dislike or not, the man must be fairly intuitive, or at least sufficiently trained to understand what is rumbling spontaneously through Max's nervous system. "Not to worry," says the aforementioned Béliard, who breaks into a half-smile while sitting at the foot of the bed, "everything will be just fine. I'll explain briefly."

It turned out from his explanation that Max was, right here and now, in transit. Right here, in other words, in a kind of specialised Orientation Centre, or so he gathered. Something like a triage area where his fate was to be decided. The time needed to rule on his case, which would be handled by a duly appointed committee, should not exceed one week, during which Max could rest and enjoy the Centre's facilities at his leisure—you'll find, incidentally, that the cuisine is excellent. As for the decisions that this committee would be handing down, their nature couldn't be simpler: there were only two possibilities, following the either/or principle. Depending on the outcome of their deliberations, Max would be sent to either one or the other of two predetermined destinations. "But don't worry," said Béliard, "each one has its good points. In any case, you'll have a better idea of what I'm talking about in five minutes. Kindly get dressed."

They left the room and headed down the corridor, along both sides of which were aligned doors identical to the one to Max's room, separated by those wall-lamps that were like little torchères of gilded wood. These unnumbered doors were closed, except for a single one, half open, that afforded a glimpse of a cell also identical to his own. It seemed that someone was cleaning it, for from behind, through the opening, Max fleetingly noticed two chambermaids in action, dressed in immaculate bodices and remarkably short black skirts, with a metal cart behind them holding an array of cleaning products and piles of clean sheets, pillowcases, flannels, and towels, as well as bundles of rumpled sheets, pillowcases, flannels, and towels, all of it under the muted whine of a vacuum cleaner and in a light perfume of deluxe disinfectant.

Then, to their left, another door opened and out came the nurse whom Max had met half an hour earlier, and who stopped at their passage. Max greeted her with a respectful nod, then turned towards Béliard, whose face tightened.

"Number 26 is rather agitated," the nurse said in a concerned voice. "I don't know what to do with him."

"Listen," Béliard said coldly, "you know perfectly well that 26 is a bit of a special case. Do you know the treatment or not?"

"Of course I know it," said the nurse, "but I've tried everything. Nothing seems to work with him."

"That's not my department," said Béliard. "That's *your* area of expertise, isn't it? Assuming you have one," he added in a cutting tone. "And besides, can't you see I'm busy? Go and see Mr Lopez if you can't handle it, maybe they'll give you a transfer. I think they might be short-handed in the kitchen. Later."

They parted without warmth. "That girl," Max ventured to remark, "she's really not bad. It's amazing how much she looks like Peggy Lee."

"She *is* Peggy Lee," Béliard said indifferently.

"Come again?" went Max.

"Yes," said Béliard. "I mean, she was Peggy Lee. Why, do you know her?"

"Well, gosh," said Max, no longer astonished by much of anything, "she was pretty famous, after all. I've seen some of her movies. And I even think I had one or two records."

"Oh, right," Béliard said indifferently, "that's true, you were in music, weren't you?"

"Not exactly the same type of music," said Max, "but even so, I was interested in other things, too. I mean other types."

He fell silent for a moment, looking at his hands, planting a diminished seventh chord in the air. "Besides, I have to admit I'm eager to get back to it," he continued. "I start to miss it pretty quickly when I'm away from my instrument."

"Ah, as for that," Béliard interrupted, "I'm afraid that's going to be a bit difficult. You'll have to reconsider the matter."

"I beg your pardon?" went Max.

"What I mean is," Béliard specified, "you're going to have to change professions. That's how it is when you come here. It's not my decision, you understand, the same rules apply to everyone."

"But what do you expect me to do?" worried Max. "I don't know how to do anything else."

"We'll find you something," said Béliard. "We find solutions for everyone. Take Peggy, for instance. She had to change jobs, too. She needed to find another trade. So fine, she chose health care, and she's not doing too badly. Besides, she has the right physique—though no matter what we do, she can't quite rid herself of her little movie-star habits. She gets like that now and again, and sometimes we have to take her down a peg."

"I see," said Max. "I thought I noticed some tension between you two."

"It's not just that," said Béliard. "It's also that I don't really like that kind of girl."

"What kind?"

"Oh," Béliard said with a wave of his hand, "big blondes and such. I know them all too well."

At the far end of the corridor they could make out a bend, past which they reached a kind of vast foyer where the light of day finally entered, pouring in through two large picture windows that faced in opposite directions. One of these windows looked out on a city that could have been a sister to Paris, as it displayed the same classic landmarks—various towers bespeaking different periods and uses, from Eiffel to Maine-Montparnasse and Jussieu, basilica, assorted monuments—but seen from very far away and on high. It wasn't possible to determine which angle they were seeing this city from, or precisely where they were, as such a view of Paris was not possible from any standpoint Max could envisage. Whatever the case, this Paris, or its twin, seemed to be smothered under a black, synthetic rain expelled by clouds of pollution, brownish and swollen like udders. The light arriving from that side was opaque, depressing, almost extinguished; whereas it flowed in gently, affectionately and brightly from the other side. This other side overlooked an immense park, a vegetal mass with soft contours forming a vast array in every shade of green, from the darkest to the most tender. Undulating at various points beneath a more clement sky, the expanse seemed to spread into infinity, as far as the eye could see, with no perceptible boundaries.

"Basically, this is what's awaiting you," said Béliard, indicating the two opposing axes. "These are the two possible orientations, you see, the park or the urban zone. You'll be assigned to one or the other. But again, don't worry, there's no bad or good solution. Both sides have their good and bad points. Anyway, as I mentioned, residence at the Centre is limited to about a week. Which means that since today's Thursday, you should be all set by next Wednesday."

"Aha," Max said unenthusiastically. "And couldn't I just stay here? It's not so bad here, I think I could get used to it. I could even help out a bit."

"That's completely out of the question," Béliard shot back. "This is just a transit station."

"Yes, but what about Peggy, for instance?" Max insisted.

"Peggy is a special case," said Béliard with an evil smile. "She's an exception. She has protection, you understand? She managed to get herself placed. The system has loopholes. Favours are done here just like anywhere else." Max didn't dare ask from whom or thanks to what Peggy Lee could enjoy such preferential treatment.

As Max, thoughtfully rubbing his chin against the grain of an already noticeable beard—which hadn't been shaved in how long, exactly? How much time separated the scene on the pavement from his awakening? Could one get information on this point?— was about to run his hand mechanically under the collar of his shirt, Béliard promptly checked his movement.

"Don't touch your wound," he said. "We're going to take care of it. On top of which," he added, knitting his brow, leaning closer to Max and examining him with a professional eye, "we'd better take care of it sooner rather than later. We can't leave you like this. In the meantime, you'd best keep to your room. You know the way."

"Yes," said Max, "but now that I think of it, I'm a bit hungry. Couldn't I have something to eat?"

"With the shape your throat is in," said Béliard, "I wouldn't advise it for the moment."

"What's wrong with my throat?" asked Max. "I don't feel anything. I feel perfectly fine."

"That's normal," said Béliard. "You're being given a special treatment until we perform the operation. You can eat afterwards. In the meantime, you're forbidden to swallow anything whatsoever; in any case, it wouldn't go through. But I'll take care of all this; someone will come and see you in a little while."

FOURTEEN

MAX WENT BACK to his room, which they had taken the trouble to clean up a little in his absence, bringing it to a relatively high-starred level of comfort. The little table now held a tray of exotic but forbidden fruit under cellophane—kiwis, mangoes, bananas, with a preponderance of papayas—plus a matching bouquet of flowers. Easy background music also played at low volume, a loop of placid, traditional, non-threatening works, no doubt selected by a middlebrow sensibility, its volume adjustable via a knob integrated into the bedside table.

As a dozen books were also piled up on the bedside table, Max examined them. They were all identically bound in reddish leatherette as if they came from the same book club, and apparently had been chosen following the same principles as the music. It was a selection of classical works: Dante and Dostoevsky, Thomas Mann and Chrétien de Troyes, things like that, despite the jarring presence of a copy of *Materialism and Empirio-Criticism* that had wandered in, and that Max leafed through for a few minutes. After he had again tried in vain to see his wound in the frosted glass of the bathroom cabinet, he decided to lie on the bed, resisting the temptation to peel a banana, abandoning Lenin to open at random *Jerusalem Delivered* in the old Auguste Desplaces translation (1840).

He didn't have time to pursue his reading very far, as someone soon knocked at his door. Béliard again, no doubt, but no, it wasn't he. It was a valet classically dressed in black and white who entered his room smiling, Good day, sir, except that in place of the habitual meal tray balancing on his open left hand, he carried a metal stem attached to a bag filled with translucent liquid, from which emerged a flexible tube ending in a needle—in other words, what is commonly called a drip.

This valet was another tall young man, with wavy, gelled black hair and a Latin smile, ironic and charming à la Dean Martin. Up close, in fact, he looked exactly like Dean Martin, down to his dancer's bearing and brown eyes sparkling with blue reflections. He bore such a resemblance to Dean Martin that Max, at the point they were at and given the precedent with Peggy Lee, began wondering if he wasn't the genuine article. Knowing that this was delicate territory, he nonetheless decided to broach it.

"I beg your pardon," he said, "but you wouldn't by any chance be Dean Martin, would you?"

"Sorry, sir, afraid not," the valet answered, his smile more Martinesque than ever. "Sad to say. I wish I were."

"It's amazing how much you look like him," Max remarked in an apologetic tone.

"So I hear," the valet smiled modestly. "People have actually told me that on more than one occasion. Now, if you would kindly roll up your sleeve. No, the right one, if you don't mind."

For the following hour, Max remained lying on his bed while a hydrating solution of glucose, vitamins, and mineral salts spread through his system. Then there was another knock on his door—God in Heaven, don't they ever stop—and this time it was again the smile of Peggy Lee, exuding more than ever an aura of vegetarianism and Christian Science. Still fresh and perky, she was followed by a young man dressed like a stretcher-bearer, who, for his part, didn't look like anyone famous. They asked Max to get undressed and to put on a kind of smock, clap a bonnet on his head, and slip on shoes made of blue synthetic fabric that crumpled like paper, then to lie down on a very tall stretcher, upon which he again set off, pushed by the young man, down the long row of corridors. This time they took the opposite direction to a service lift as huge as in a hospital, as fast as in a skyscraper: they must have been descending at top speed from a very high altitude, since from the heights of his stretcher Max had to force himself to swallow several times to open his eardrums, blocked by the race down to Basement Level 3.

Then new corridors flooded with white light and pierced by wide swinging doors, one of which opened on to an operating room that was no different from any other operating room; nor did the surgeon call to mind any celebrity. "Just a little repair job," the doctor explained, planting another needle in Max's forearm—the left one this time. "We're going to fix you up with a small cosmetic procedure, since of course vital functions are no longer an issue." It would just be a matter of cleaning the wound, sewing up the pieces of his lacerated throat, then reconstructing the damaged elements, especially around the spinal cord—a delicate area—before plugging up and masking the hole created by his attacker's weapon. Max plunged into chemical sleep before the other had finished his explanations.

He awoke with a start, took a moment to recognise his room, but immediately identified Peggy Lee at his bedside, sitting on a chair and flipping through the pages of a magazine. As he was opening his mouth to ask a question, she gently placed her right hand on his lips, posing on her own a finger of the left. "Don't try to talk," she said softly, "it's too soon, it could hurt. But don't worry; it will go very quickly from now on. In your condition, it heals pretty fast. You'll see, you'll feel better by tomorrow." Although he didn't understand a word of what she was saying, Max nodded with a knowing air, glanced briefly at the IV that was lodged once more in his right arm, then dropped off to sleep again like a stone.

The next time he opened his eyes, there was no-one in his room, which he now recognised instantly. No sound came from anywhere: they must have disconnected the background music to ensure that he get some rest. No way to know what time it was, evening or morning, day or night. For lack of anything else to do, Max reviewed all the information he had gathered since arriving at the Centre, making a synthesis, then reflecting on what was now liable to happen to him—what zone they were going to assign him to. By all appearances, aesthetically speaking, the park seemed to be a good solution, even if it would be smart to check it out more closely. Since Béliard had indicated the decision would be made by studying his file, Max visualised the future with optimism, having a fair amount of confidence in the balance sheet of his life.

For it seemed to him that he had always behaved rather well. Taking a survey of his existence, he came to the conclusion that he hadn't seriously lapsed in any domain whatsoever. Naturally, he had suffered from doubt, alcoholism, and acedia; naturally, he had occasionally succumbed to laziness, allowed himself a few minor tantrums, or indulged in bouts of pride, but what else could he have done? Overall, it all seemed decidedly venial. If one was granted access to the park based on one's merits, Max couldn't really see what might stand in the way of his acceptance, but it was no doubt premature to speculate on his fate before getting more information—and at that moment, the door opened to reveal Béliard.

FIFTEEN

"WELL," PROFFERED BÉLIARD in the martial tones of a senior consultant, "how are we feeling this morning?" So it was morning. The next day, unless it was the day after that. But before Max had a chance to answer, someone knocked at the door: this time it was the valet carrying an actual meal tray.

"You've noticed everything moves very quickly here," noted Béliard, handing Max a pocket mirror. "Don't even need a bandage, the healing is almost done." And in fact, in the mirror, Max saw at the base of his throat only a slight pale line bordered by a barely perceptible row of dots. "You're going to be able to start eating again," Béliard added, pointing to the valet, who promptly cleared the table before setting down the tray, then busied himself with removing the IV. After extracting the needle from Max's forearm, he briefly swabbed the area with alcohol, the swipe of a dust cloth over a waxed canvas, and zip zip zip, a little square of sticking plaster on top, and end of story. "There," said Béliard, "that's taken care of. Now you can get dressed."

"It's just a light meal, sir," the valet apologised under his breath as Max slipped on his shirt. "Because of your operation. A little convalescent diet, not very exciting, I grant, and I sincerely hope you won't hold it against us. You'll soon be able to enjoy more varied menus." In fact, this one consisted of white rice and steamed vegetables, a slice of boiled ham, yogurt, and fruit compote, washed down with mineral water. "Will this be to your liking?" worried the valet, while meticulously arranging the silverware in parentheses around the dish.

"Cut it short, Dino, cut it short," exclaimed Béliard, who seemed to derive great pleasure from bossing the junior staff around. He tried to dismiss the domestic abruptly, the moment the latter had finished his task, but Dino, since Dino he was, took his sweet time with a distant, smiling, indifferent, calm indolence.

"Now that you're recovered," said Béliard, "I'll show you around the place a bit." They took the same lift that had carried Max to the operating room and, as they went down, Max tried to worm some information out of Béliard about Dino.

"Why?" the other asked coldly.

"I don't know," said Max, "I like that young man. I find him very pleasant, even rather special."

"I can't answer that," said Béliard. "He doesn't like people talking about him. He prefers not to have anything known about him personally, which I respect. People have this right in our institution. But I won't hide the fact that he annoys me sometimes. Truth be told, I find him a bit too casual."

This time, the lift stopped three floors above the surgical level, at the ground floor of the Centre. They followed a new network of corridors, wider, better decorated—fresh bouquets of flowers on console-tables, neoclassical statuettes on pedestals, fantastical landscapes—and more populated—chambermaids and factotums, secretaries wearing glasses and buns who, hugging their folders under their arms, gave Béliard timid and respectful greetings when crossing his path, which he vaguely answered with a brief movement of his chin. Corridors and more corridors that finally ended at a gigantic foyer lit *a giorno* by gleaming crystal-and-bronze chandeliers framed by oblong pastel windows, and from which rose a monumental staircase with two revolutions. "Here we are," said Béliard. "This is the entrance of the Centre." Past a revolving door one could in fact make out, punctuated by water fountains and clumps of vegetation, the kind of vast stretch of gravel that one often sees in front of grand mansions—usually strewn with long motor cars, stained by oil from their sumps, and furrowed with traces of their tyres, but here, as far as Max could tell from where he stood, there was no stain, no trace of any tyre, no car beneath the clear sky.

Nor did there appear to be a security guard on duty inside the foyer or in the surrounding area. No sentinel, no watchman, not a single video camera, ah, wait, there's something: hidden behind the architecture of the staircase, Max spotted a small, discreet booth, in frosted glass to waist level and containing a desk, behind which a sexagenarian dressed in traditional grand hotel concierge garb—black frock coat over white waistcoat, his lapel sporting two crossed keys—seemed to be in a dream, oblivious to the world.

"It doesn't look like you have a very large staff," Max observed. "People can come and go as they please, can they?"

"It's not quite that simple," Béliard moderated, "but it's a little like that. We work on the honour system, if you like. Surveillance is very low-level, everyone is responsible for himself. I'll show you around the park tomorrow, if that sounds all right. In the meantime, let me introduce you to the director. Would you like to meet him?"

"Oh, yes," said Max, "good idea. I'd like to meet the director."

"Let me make sure he's in," said Béliard, setting off towards the concierge's booth. "Good morning, Joseph, is Mr Lopez in his office at the moment?"

At Joseph's affirmative reply, they took the staircase, on the landings of which several bellboys stood or circulated—very young subjects, barely pubescent, dressed in woollen dolman jackets and striped trousers, white collars, gloves, and caps, and engaged in apparently farcical activities that Max and Béliard's passage momentarily disrupted. On the second floor was a large double door guarded by an usher who, with a grave salute to Béliard, let them pass. They crossed through a string of vast rooms that were sometimes empty, sometimes sectioned off into cubicles separated by glass partitions behind which, here and there, one could make out a silhouette bent over its job. After they had crossed another antechamber, Béliard knocked on the next door, which immediately opened on to a huge directorial office. We'll choose not to describe this office in much detail; let us simply note that its furnishings and decorations matched—perhaps in a slightly duller and sadder way, and a little less well maintained—the style of the rooms Max had thus far walked through.

Directorial or not, the office was occupied only by one thin, stooped, standing man, bent over thick bundles of yellowish documents spread out over a desk. This person was of average height, tightly dressed in inexpensive grey. His long, waxy face denoted a poorly balanced diet; his rheumy eyes were tearful. He sported the anxious air of an underpaid clerk, depressive, apologetic more than displeased about being so anxious, but resigned to it. He must have been a secretary or accountant, or one of the undersecretaries or under-accountants working for the director, whom he was, no doubt, going out to notify.

Or maybe not. "Mr Lopez," Béliard uttered gently and with deference, "this is Mr Delmarc, who has recently joined us. He was admitted this week and he wanted to meet you."

"Ah," the other said confusedly, raising an intimidated eye towards Max, "well, welcome." He did not even ask Max a few questions for form's sake. At first glance, he seemed a bit frightened; his questioning look made him appear overwhelmed by events—although one might wonder if this wasn't some kind of ruse, a trick he used so as to be left in peace; if in fact he knew, better than anyone, all about Max. "What did you say his name was?" he asked Béliard, who repeated Max's last name for him, spelling it out. "Yes," said Lopez, "I see. Just a moment." Bending once more over the desk and rifling through the scattered documents, he eventually pulled one out and handed it to Béliard. The latter first skimmed it rapidly, then, in the general silence, began rereading it more closely.

Standing at a cautious distance, Max nonetheless glanced over at the object. It was a rectangular, lined index card, 5 x 8 format, its edges yellowed and slightly frayed, almost entirely covered in a fine, close handwriting traced in brown ink: apparently it was not of recent vintage, like most of the documents piled up on Lopez's desk. It was reminiscent of those other index cards that people used to consult in public libraries, before their catalogues went digital.

"Hey," Max allowed himself to observe, "you aren't computerised here?"

"Did I ask you anything?" Béliard answered without raising his eyes.

Meanwhile, Lopez had sat down, brushing imaginary dust with the back of his hand from the surface of his desk, which he stared at vacantly. Then Béliard, having finished reading, glanced quickly at Max before handing the card back to Lopez. "Right," he said, "I think I basically get the picture."

"What's the matter with them?" Max asked himself. "What's there to see, in particular?"

Two fried eggs were waiting for him in his room, accompanied by a beer and a slice of melon, the first discreet sign of an improvement. As of the next day, in fact, his lunch would offer more depth, then dinner would be frankly worthy of a five-star restaurant. Max had to spend that entire second post-operative day in his room, leafing through the books he had, but without enthusiasm and not really able to read, at first distracted by anxiety over the index card he'd seen in Lopez's office, then, as of early afternoon, more profoundly distracted by boredom. Dino still handled the service with his smiling and detached discretion, although it was still impossible to make him be anything but even-spoken; then Béliard came by for coffee. When evening fell, Max fretted to him about his schedule in the days to come.

"It's just that I'm starting to go a bit crazy here," he had to admit. "Couldn't I just go out for a little walk now and then?"

"But you're absolutely free," Béliard assured him. "Your door is open. At this point, nothing is stopping you from coming and going as you please in the establishment. As for distractions *per se*, we'll see about that later. Cigar?"

SIXTEEN

THE START of the next day would prove to be pretty depressing. It's just that it was Sunday and, even in a place as cut off from the world as the Centre, Sunday produced, as always and everywhere, its effect of indolence and emptiness, of pale expanse and hollow, sorrowful resonance. First there would be an interminable morning, during which Max would keep to his room, pondering the matter of Lopez's index card, until somebody served him one of those cold meals that you get when there's no-one in the kitchen. Besides, it wasn't even properly served to him: when he started feeling hungry and opened his door to watch for Dino's arrival, he found the tray set down in the corridor at his feet like a doormat. And Béliard, like Dino, was no doubt taking advantage of his weekly day off, unless he already had lunch plans, since he didn't show up for his daily coffee with Max. Max now felt fully recovered from his operation and, once fed, he decided to take a spin around the Centre. With a little idea in the back of his mind.

It wouldn't exactly be easy. He had to reconstruct, by himself, the path he and Béliard had taken the day before. Emptier even than usual, the corridor on his floor gave off the glacial echo of a deserted boarding-school during holidays, when all the others have gone to be with their families and you remain behind, alone with the staff, whether out of punishment or orphanhood. Except that Max didn't come across any staff. He could have sworn he made out the rumbling of a vacuum cleaner in the distance, the dim clanks of a mop in an empty pail but, as there was no-one to be seen, these could just as easily have been slight auditory hallucinations produced by the silence itself. He had no trouble finding the lift and, once its doors had closed behind him, as the mechanism made no sound, Max was shut into a higher silence, a silence within the silence, a cubed silence that didn't bespeak anything good. It was with a troubled index finger that he took aim and pressed the button for the ground floor; then the descent was long enough for his entire life to pass before him, until the concluding *dring* of the lift brought him back with a slight start.

As on the day before, the lift doors opened on to the same network of hallways that were better decorated than upstairs. The rooms from yesterday were now deserted, and Max could linger at the doorways, looking at what must have been offices, exhibit halls, and conference rooms furnished with coffee machines. He ventured into what looked like a reception hall, a huge space whose decoration suggested a vaguely Soviet aesthetic: stucco and mouldings, thick damask curtains, carpets with indistinct designs, and large ungainly furniture, heavy with good will and coiffed with table mats. At the far end of the room, there was even a piano. A concert grand. Well, well.

Seeing it, Max realised that for the past several days he had almost forgotten about music. And yet music was his life, or at least it had been. But he had hardly even mentioned it to Béliard, just long enough for the latter to intimate that he would now have to give it up. Max remembered, moreover, that he hadn't been particularly devastated by this news at the time, but the piano, well after all. A piano. Max approached it very slowly, as one might draw near a wild animal, as if the instrument were threatening to fly off with a squawk at the slightest sudden movement. Taking advantage of Béliard's dominical absence, he felt the desire to see what this model had under its hood, the urge to make it talk. But first, prudently halting a few feet away, he tried to make out its label. Neither Gaveau nor Steinway nor Bechstein nor Bösendorfer nor anything: no signature on the gold plate under the music desk. A big, anonymous machine, black, sleek, shining, solitary, and closed. Inching closer on tiptoe, Max silently turned his hands supine but, when he gently risked the tips of his fingers towards the instrument to open the fall board, he noticed that it was locked, making the keys inaccessible. Max insisted, trying to force the cover, but no, nothing doing, it was bolted. Bernie, among his many talents, would have been perfectly capable of prying open the lock in two beats of three movements, but there was no more Bernie. Bernie, too, had been his life.

Max had to be content with circling for a moment, not more than two or three times, around the closed piano. Without much conviction, he also tried to lift the instrument's lid, if only to examine its sounding board and wrest plank, caress the strings and run his fingernails over them like a harp, but in vain: locked shut like the rest. During these two or three turns around the piano, the little idea grew in the back of Max's mind.

This idea led him to retrace fairly quickly and easily the path towards the main entrance. He moved forward in the same thick silence that, not merely amplifying the sound of his steps, also brought forth other various and indistinct sounds, distant moans and grunts, whines, creaks, and buzzings that stopped dead the moment Max became aware of their untraceable origin, their possible genesis inside him, his cranium acting as their echo chamber. When he found himself back in the foyer, it was equally devoid of any guard: even the concierge was absent from his glass booth. Max nonetheless made a show of examining the place as nonchalantly as you please, distracted but exhibiting a complete curiosity, like a tourist set loose in a chateau without his guide, coming and going with no discernible method on open-house day. Nevertheless, a goal directed his wanderings: to amble closer, by concentric circles and oh so casually, to the foyer's revolving door; and then, having reached it, to give it a slight prod to make sure it wasn't blocked; then, this being verified, to push it more firmly, slip into its space, and stroll out as naturally as could be. He experienced a brief sensation of claustrophobia when he found himself, for the space of three seconds, enclosed in the door's rotating airlock, while the once little idea now left the back of his mind to swell and invade his head completely—I'm getting out of here, God help me, I'm getting the hell out of here.

To go where? No idea. Once outside, the main thing was to get as far away as possible; after that, we'd see. The exterior consisted of a minimal landscape: past the gravelled esplanade that stretched before the Centre, a summarily tarmacked pathway opened up, its pavement gradually splitting into plates of asphalt that were increasingly unconnected, among which grew tufts of weeds. This pathway soon became a stony dirt road, barely suitable for traffic and lined by dry shrubs with outlines like stick insects, with nothing in sight but sterile undulations on either side, stretching to infinity.

Nothing in this landscape suggested either of the ones Max had seen from the windows: it was an intermediate stage, grey, neutral, and chilly in nature. Max decided to follow this dirt road, shivering a little, and in any case having no choice, nor the slightest idea of where he was going. After roughly five hundred yards, he thought to turn around and get a look at the Centre. It was, as the lift had defined it from within, a very tall building, almost a skyscraper, about forty storeys high, grey in colour and flanked with long, low wings and annexes. The whole thing must have been able to house a huge number of people.

He walked another mile or two along this deserted road in the middle of the countryside before he made out the faint whine of a rather shrill engine, no doubt a two-stroke, slowly growing louder behind him. Max took pains to act as if there were nothing untoward until he heard the engine slow down right near him, behind his back, humming gently in neutral. At that point he had to turn around and look: it was a service vehicle of a model unfamiliar to Max—moreover, as with the piano, no manufacturer's mark was visible. Halfway between a Mini Moke and a golf trolley, it was a small, topless, all-purpose conveyance, rather stylish in its very simplicity. Max had no trouble recognising Dino sitting behind the wheel, even though he'd swapped his valet's livery for a well-cut electric-blue business suit. He was also wearing a hat that he pushed back slightly while opening the passenger door with the other hand, not saying a word but grinning irresistibly with the full range of his enamel.

It was clear that there was no discussion to be had; Max could only get in quietly and sit down. Dino manoeuvred the vehicle and they set off with no comment towards the Centre, at first in silence. Then, as if sensing that this silence might begin to weigh on them, Dino began delicately humming a melody that Max immediately identified: "The Night Is Young and You're So Beautiful"; then he started to sing it for real, with lyrics, at half-volume, while improvising a rhythm section by tapping his fingers on the steering wheel. Not only did Max recognise the song, but he recognised more and more precisely the timbre of Dino's voice—that crooner's voice, a bit ironic, nonchalant, and gifted, but aware and making fun of its own nonchalance: obviously Dean Martin, of course Dean Martin. It was no less indisputable than it was intimidating—because, after all, Dean Martin.

But it was also a chance to know the artist a little better, even while not letting on that he'd been recognised, the other having made it very clear that he wished to remain incognito. If Dino didn't want to be identified, that was his business, and Max wasn't going to pester him about it. Still, they could talk a bit, broach a host of other subjects, like, well, I don't know.

"Dino," he said once the other had finished singing, "would you like to have a drink one of these days? I'd enjoy getting to know you better."

The other, who up until now had been nothing but relaxed and friendly, suspended his smile for an instant, albeit without hostility, and, turning politely towards Max, he answered calmly, "No-one can know me, sir," before redeploying his dazzling whites. Max took care not to insist: Dino was a tranquil and secretive man, and as Béliard had said, one had to respect that.

As they drove towards the Centre beneath a sky that was almost as white as that smile, Max began to ponder the awful trouble that was surely awaiting him on his return. He could hardly imag-

ine the disciplinary measures that might follow his attempt to
run away or escape—the very nature of his crime was still to be
defined—but there must be a punishment for such conduct.
What? Penitence, imprisonment, reprimands, forced labour, appearance before a disciplinary committee followed by expulsion
pure and simple—although where could they expel him to? And
yet, for the moment, none of this seemed worth worrying about
to judge by Dino, who continued to tap his fingers casually on the
steering wheel—although it wasn't really sympathy that emanated
from his behaviour, more like he didn't seem to give a damn, and
more generally didn't seem to give a damn about anything, and
not only seemed, at that.

Still, arriving back at the Centre, Max was not greeted by a row
of impassive armed guards or nurses brandishing syringes, nor
dragged to a jail cell or before an assembly of men in black. Dino
merely accompanied him back to his room, where Béliard, sitting
on the single bed, was waiting calmly while looking at his watch.
Max feared remonstrations or even threats, for on top of everything else, he had probably ruined Béliard's Sunday, his one day
off all week—but no, the other proved to be as benevolent and
detached as Dino. And even fairly thoughtful. As Max was about
to launch into jumbled explanations, Béliard pre-empted him
with a wave of his hand.

"Don't worry about it," he said. "Everyone has tried at some
point. Well, not exactly everybody," he qualified. "But you know,
we don't really have anything against this kind of initiative. On

97

the contrary, it's very healthy, it's a good reaction. It's especially a sign that you're completely healed. And now, if you'd be good enough to get your belongings ready," he added with a circular gesture.

"I don't have any belongings," Max reminded him, worried.

"Forgive me," said Béliard, "it was just an expression. It's only that you're going to change lodgings."

Max was still expecting the worst—dark dungeon, padded cell, cooler—but instead, no, not at all, it seemed that they had even decided to upgrade him. Located on the same floor, larger and especially better lit than the first, his new room included double French doors leading to a balcony, from which one could enjoy an unimpeded view of the park. That evening, Max would again have dinner in his room, and Béliard, having invited him to lunch at the restaurant the next day, lent him a pair of binoculars thanks to which Max, while the daylight lasted, could get an overall idea of how the park was laid out.

Bringing Max's tray, Dino, who was attired in his livery once more, marvelled at the new room, sparing no praise for the furnishings, the functional arrangement, and the colour of the walls. "It's much better than my place," he observed. "And just look at that view. Wow!"

Uttering this interjection, he looked so much like what he obviously was that Max, no longer able to stand it, cried out, "Come on, Dino, please, I'm begging you, just admit who you are."

"Who I am?" The valet darkened.

"You know perfectly well what I mean," Max said, exasperated. "I'm sure it's you. I know you, I've often seen you in the movies, I even saw you in a Tashlin film on TV not more than a month ago. I owned some of your records. Come on, admit it, it'll be our secret."

"Sir," Dino declared firmly, "I like you, but I would appreciate it if you did not bring this subject up again. O.K.?"

SEVENTEEN

THE NEXT DAY at around half-past twelve, Béliard came to find
Max, saying it was time to socialise him a bit. "It's not good for
you to stay all alone in your little corner; you can't keep yourself
cut off from the world. A little conversation never hurts." This
would therefore be Max's first meal outside his room, at the door
of which they met Peggy in the corridor. There she was, apparently just hanging around with nothing special to do, as if she
were just waiting to run into Max. And although he, as we have
said before, had never exactly been what you'd call a seducer, never
been sensitive to the more or less subliminal signals that might
have been addressed to him, since he was never sure enough of
himself to consider them such, it seemed to him that Peggy
looked at him more closely, smiled at him more acutely. Even her
make-up and her gait, suppler and more light-footed than usual,
weren't the same as the other times, as if something—well, who

knows. Anyway, what are you rambling about? Who do you think you're fooling?

"It's not the only restaurant in the Centre, of course, but this one isn't bad," Béliard announced, leading Max through yet another network of corridors that this time did not pass by the lift doors. "Otherwise we could never manage," he continued. "In fact, there's one on every floor. We're divided into sectors, you see, with people grouped by geographical area. The ones you're about to see didn't live very far from your neighbourhood. You might even run across some fellows you knew. In any case, they're only here for a week, like you."

"Fine," said Max, "but why only fellows?"

"Ah," went Béliard, "I neglected to mention that the Centre isn't co-ed. The women's section is somewhere else. I know that sounds a bit old-fashioned. The point has been hotly debated with the management team, but for the moment that's how things stand. We'll see. We have time. We have all the time in the world. Besides, here we are. After you; I insist."

They entered a space able to contain some two or three hundred persons, sitting around about forty tables that were each set for six. There were mainly elderly men, of course, who ate slowly and little without looking around, but there were also some younger ones, sometimes of Max's age, who gaily asked for more wine. Among the latter, one could count a higher proportion of accident victims, murder victims, and suicides who for the most part exhibited souvenirs of serious injuries—puncture wounds, impacts from projectiles, traces of strangulation, and skull fractures. Of course, the surgeons must have treated these lesions as they had operated on Max's, making their scars barely visible, but nonetheless some of these stigmata remained distinguishable and, depending on how each man looked, one could have made up a game of guessing what had happened. Whatever the case, past events did not seem to ruin the appetite of any of them. "Well," said Béliard, "I'll leave you now. You'll be taken care of, and I'll see you later."

A headwaiter in fact came up to them, leading Max to a table where a free seat was available. As Max didn't recognise any of his tablemates at first glance, and as none of them took the initiative to speak to him, he used the opportunity to study the place, and after it the staff. It was, then, a room of huge proportions, monumental angles, and vast perspectives, but in no way reminiscent of a refectory, mess hall, or company cafeteria. On the contrary, everything suggested the decor of a very expensive restaurant: pleated curtains, loaded chandeliers, cataracts of hanging green plants, immaculate embroidered napkins and tablecloths, heavy engraved silverware, prismatic knife-rests, fine porcelain monogrammed with indecipherable interlacing, gleaming crystal, and guilloched carafes, with small copper lamps and assorted bouquets on each table.

The service was supervised by a headwaiter wearing a black dinner jacket, starched shirt with wing collar, black bow tie and white waistcoat, black socks, and matt black shoes with rubber heels. He was assisted by front of house waiters in black evening coats, waistcoats, and trousers, starched shirts with wing collars, black bow ties, black socks, and matt black shoes with rubber heels. These latter oversaw a brigade of assistant waiters in white chequered spencer jackets, buttoned-up black waistcoats, black trousers, starched white shirts with wing collars, white bow ties, black socks, and matt black shoes with rubber heels. As for the sommeliers who constantly verified the levels in each glass, they wore black tailcoats, waistcoats, and trousers, starched white shirts with wing collars, black bow ties, and aprons of heavy black cloth with patch pockets and leather strings; an insignia depicting a gilded bunch of grapes was pinned to the left lapel of the tailcoat.

Lower down in the hierarchy, servers assisted by attendants provided the link between the tables in the service of their assistant waiter and the kitchens, unseen areas in which, under the authority of a head chef, as in any worthy establishment, there must have been an army of sauce cooks, pastry chefs, coffee makers, silver polishers, dishwashers, glass washers, cellarmen, wine stewards, and fruit arrangers—and at the top of the pyramid, gliding along the margins of the tables and keeping a wary eye out for trouble, the restaurant manager was wearing a jacket and waistcoat of grey fabric with black flecks, a starched white shirt and collar, a grey tie, striped trousers, black socks, black shoes, and impeccably silver hair.

No doubt having arrived at the Centre before Max, thus necessarily better informed, the fellows around the tables seemed much more knowledgeable than he about their two possible destinations, park or urban zone, each one wondering about his own fate without neglecting to comment, sometimes rather cattily, on that of the others. They were speculating high stakes, bets were placed under the table, and Max listened. Before learning of the gender segregation, he had briefly nurtured the ever-possible idea of finding Rose at that restaurant, but let's not go into that. Let it pass.

Since the stays lasted a week, some, already there for the past five or six days, had had time to start conversations and had got to know the others. Max felt like the new boy who needed to be broken in. They passed him the salt without a glance and barely said a word to him. It seemed that the only glimmer of sympathy he received was from the meat carver in immaculate kitchen togs who, circulating among the tables with his little chrome cart, sliced the roasts to each diner's specifications after having presented to each the various cuts: it seemed that the choices that day were spring chicken à la Polonaise or saddle of venison with Cumberland sauce. Once he had opted for the spring chicken, Max consumed what was on his menu, including coffee, simply waiting for Béliard to come to fetch him.

Later, in the lift: "So," asked Béliard, "did you run into anyone you know?"

"No," answered Max, who, having spotted no familiar faces in the restaurant, but whom the presence of Peggy and Dino at the Centre—even if the latter clung to his anonymity—had impressed, hinted at his disappointment in not meeting other celebrities.

"On that score, you needn't waste your time," said Béliard, who explained that, while one of the Centre's principles was to recycle old personalities as part of the staff, there were nonetheless quotas to be respected. The whole thing was carefully regulated: no more than two per floor. "For instance, on the next level down," he specified, "they've got Renato Salvatori and Soraya." Some of these past luminaries found themselves exempted from the choice between urban zone and park and were appointed permanently. Their status was without risk, of course, but also without much of a future.

Max was about to have him develop this point about the future when the lift's discreet bell notified them that they had arrived. We won't elaborate on the new corridors that led, this time, to an entrance vastly different from the one through which Max had tried to escape. Here, there was no revolving door reminiscent of an old colonial hotel, no booth, no vista on to a gravelled courtyard: here, two high, wide glass doors led straight out to nature.

"Come on," said Béliard. "Follow me. A little after-dinner stroll, what do you say?"

"With pleasure," said Max.

To begin with, they climbed up a hill from which Max could view the overall structure of the park. It was a huge verdant expanse, roughly circular in shape, but of such vastness that a tour of its horizon seemed to exceed the usual three hundred and sixty degrees. It was composed of remarkably varied landscapes, felicitously combined, a montage of every imaginable geomorphological entity—valleys, hills, steep slopes, canyons, plateaux, peaks, and so on—among which snaked a very complex hydrographic network: here and there, transient or fixed, areas of brilliance revealed or suggested rivers, streams, lakes, ponds, basins, spouts, waterfalls, and reflecting pools, at the horizon of which one could make out a seashore.

Once they had arrived back at the foot of the hill, Max saw a green profusion begin to stretch towards that horizon, a concert of trees and plants in which cohabited every species growing in the most varied climates—pine juxtaposing elm and yew rubbing against terebinth—as one sees in certain Portuguese gardens, but much more exhaustive, to the point where not one of the thirty thousand varieties of trees inventoried in the world seemed to be missing.

"Let's keep going," said Béliard. "We'll take a closer look."

They embarked on a path of a style quite different from the one Max had taken the day before, abundantly floral, bordered by fruit, ornamental and forest trees, and prickly, intertwined vines. In the heart of this vast flora, of course, the fauna was not to be outdone. Rabbits bolted in the bushes like furtive little machines; flights of iridescent hummingbirds striated the sky between the branches; and at mid-level buzzed de luxe insects, hand-picked— varnished dragonflies, lacquered ladybirds, metallic beetles. Further on, certain ill-mannered monkeys hung from the vines screeching like morons while other monkeys, calmer and better disciplined, gathered fruit in the pear trees, the handles of lovely wicker baskets nestled in the crooks of their elbows.

After a while, and seemingly at a great distance, small houses set far apart could be distinguished among the trees that were equally varied in appearance. These constructions bespoke various cultural origins, from traditional hut to yurt and from isba to tea pavilion, but one could also make out more modernist edifices, gas-inflatable structures, concrete dwellings with glass appendages, one-piece abodes of diverse materials, monoshell capsules made of plastic, and even a prefab bungalow. Every one of them had two peculiarities. First, each one was of reduced size, designed to house one or two people at most; and second, each one seemed as if it could be quickly dismantled and rebuilt at short notice, when they weren't simply mounted on wheels. Seeing Max's surprise, Béliard explained that geographical mobility was a way of life among park occupants, a nomadism encouraged by its ample dimensions. Scattered throughout the landscape, these mobile structures generally stood at a decent remove from one another, although certain more sedentary residences, installed in the tree branches, might form a network linked by suspended catwalks, running from plane tree to sequoia. But Max could only see these houses, in which one occasionally glimpsed an occupant or two, from too far away to really make them out in any detail.

"Couldn't we get a little closer?" he asked.

"No," answered Béliard, "we can't. We mustn't disturb them, they don't like that. They value their privacy. And besides, you have visitor status, you see. I can't let you mix with the residents. I can tell you in any case that they're comfortable, all of them at home in their own little spaces, which they designed themselves. It's a very popular solution. Since the park is so vast, they can live here in peace, without being on top of each other. But sometimes they get together. They have the use of sporting equipment. There are golf courses, tennis courts, yacht clubs, the works. I have to say, the amenities aren't bad. They also organise small concerts from time to time, little shows, though of course no-one is required to attend. Everyone does as they please. Actually, I *can* take you to visit one of the units from closer up. We can go and have a look; it's unoccupied at the moment."

He guided Max towards a minuscule English-style cottage flanked by a modest garden teeming with roses and anemones, phlox and love-in-a-mist, cleomes and poppies, under fleeting rainbows unfurled by the automatic sprinkler system, in the shadow of mastic and sweet gum trees. "Just look how lovely that is," marvelled Béliard, "they can even tend their gardens. And besides, there are as many fruit trees as you could want in the park, you see, you can eat anything you like. Well, when I say 'anything', in reality it's mainly papaya. There are practically no seasons here, the climate is ideal. So it grows constantly, papaya, it never stops. Just between you and me, it helps if you like papayas—personally, I have trouble digesting them. But here, let's have a look at some more exotic houses. We'll take advantage of the fact that no-one's in them right now. No surprise, really, since they aren't nearly as comfortable. They mainly serve as stop-overs."

And so Max was able to admire, by turns: a lodge built on oak pillars, with chestnut beams and willow poles, the whole thing thatched with layers of pine needles arranged on a wicker trellis; a circular cabin whose frame, walls, and roof were formed of interlaced reeds, bamboo, and rushes; a low-lying shed covered with palm fronds woven together with goat's wool, and in which the heavy canvas of the walls and roof were stretched and held in place by thick, braided cords; a conical hut with A-shaped rafters built on layers of brick that were coated with a mortar composed of mud, mashed grass, and horse manure, and bonded together with a cement made of peat and cowpats.

"I grant it all smacks a bit of a natural history museum," admitted Béliard. "It's fairly ethnographic. That's enough of these. But you also have less exotic things, look over there." Max in fact noticed, as they walked, miniature Mediterranean villas, fishermen's cottages, workers' units, and even, still more roughly assembled, refurbished caravans, estate cars, or mini-vans, customised bunkers and blockhouses, and inverted boat hulls. "You see," said Béliard, "there's a little of everything. Whatever the client wants."

"Yes," said Max. "And how are they heated?"

"The climate is carefully regulated," Béliard smiled. "You don't need heating here, ever, any more than you need fans. Anyway, there it is," he concluded. "This was just to give you some idea of the park; in any case you'll be assigned tomorrow. But you can see how comfortable you'd be, no?"

"Oh yes," recognised Max. "The only thing is, I'd be a little afraid of boredom."

"Ah," said Béliard, "there's the rub, of course. Right. Well, it's getting late, time to be heading back."

As he was returning to his new room, Max again ran into Peggy in the corridor. She stopped alongside him, all smiles, will you be needing anything? "Everything's fine," Max assured her, "everything's just fine."

"So, you were able to visit the park, you saw how pretty it is?"

"Magnificent," certified Max, "truly gorgeous."

"Well, I'll let you go, I've finished my shift," Peggy indicated, "so I'll say goodnight."

"Goodnight," said Max, "goodnight."

They parted company with prolonged smiles, intent looks. Max hadn't been in his room three minutes when there was a knock at his door. It was Peggy again, who entered on a flimsy

pretext, claiming that the chambermaids had left something behind, looking for that something in vain, then turning impetu-
ously towards Max and, against all odds, rushing into his arms.
And that was how Max Delmarc, one fine evening, possessed
Peggy Lee.

EIGHTEEN

NIGHT OF LOVE with Peggy Lee

NINETEEN

THE NEXT MORNING, Max woke up very late and alone in his bed. As he turned over, eyes still shut, the first spontaneous movement of his brain was to recall the previous night. At first, the episode with Peggy seemed so highly improbable that he suspected it was just a dream. But once he opened his eyes, then sat up with a start and gave his sheets a quick once-over, the state they were in confirmed the reality of the facts. He fell back again, pulling the covers over himself and letting out a contented sigh. Then, after revisiting the high points of the evening, came the second movement of his brain: it was today, he remembered. It was today, according to Béliard, that he would be informed of his fate.

In anticipation of the verdict, Max attempted once again to take stock of his life, as he had done after his operation but in a more strictly canonical fashion: exhaustive examination of conscience following the accepted protocol. Let us recapitulate, then: I've never killed anyone, practically never stolen anything, no memory of bearing false witness, and I rarely swore. I always made sure to rest on the Sabbath, and as for my parents, I think I did the best I could. While I never had a chance to explore the question of adultery very fully, there was certainly the more general matter of coveting my neighbour's goods, wives included, on which I perhaps haven't always been entirely above-board. But fine, nothing excessive. Then, of course, there's the problem of divinity, which I believe I handled reasonably well. Sceptical but honest. Hesitant but respectful. Apart from that, I really can't think of anything. I admit I sometimes had occasion to drink excessively, but first of all, given my profession, I think there were extenuating circumstances, and besides, it seems to me that nothing in the Ten Commandments directly addresses the question of alcohol. What else? Overall I believe I can say that I behaved, yes, rather well. It should be fine. It should go smoothly. Although the park, well, I don't know that it appeals all that much, but we'll see.

Basically satisfied with this panorama, Max then re-projected the film of his night with Peggy. She really was pretty amazing sexually, very imaginative as far as he could judge—he who, for lack of experience, since he had never known much in his life other than two or three unhappy love affairs and a few call girls, could only suppose that she had in fact been full of ideas. Even though in this domain one can rarely surpass the ten or twelve possible deployments with their many variations; after that, it's always pretty much the same thing. For example, during a good

part of the night, she had performed long and remarkably so-
phisticated blow jobs that Max, back when he would listen to her
singing, would never have imagined she could conceive of, despite
her artistic talent. He would never have thought of her that way.

It was a little before noon and he, still in bed, was at this point
in his reflections when Béliard entered his room with an unaccustomed albeit very discreet look on his face, halfway between
reprobation and amusement. "Is everything O.K.?" asked Béliard.
"Did you sleep well?"

"Not bad," answered Max, wondering if by some chance the
other could know about the details of his night.

"Good," Béliard said abruptly. "I have your results. I've come
to give you the report; they ruled this morning."

"Go ahead," said Max.

"I'm terribly sorry," said Béliard, "but you're being sent to the
urban zone."

"Well, all right," said Max, wondering again if by chance his
night with Peggy might have weighed in the verdict, constituting
an infraction of the non-co-ed principle that might, just as easily,
extend to a more generalised intolerance of sexuality. Just as easily. Still, despite the slight reticence he had exhibited about the
park—which was in fact only a bit of coyness, based on his cer-
tainty that he'd been assigned there automatically—anxiety
seized him. When you got down to it, they hadn't really told him
anything about the urban zone, and besides, what was so special
about that idiotic name that they'd taken from an old *métro* map?

"To be honest, I don't really understand," he said. "It seems unfair. With the life I lived, my devotion to art, I thought I could expect a little more indulgence."

"You know," Béliard softened, "I won't deny that there's always some measure of subjectivity in these deliberations. It's not automatic. It often happens like this, it's almost standard practice. And besides, we have to maintain the quotas," he added without further details.

"And there isn't any way," Max coughed, "there isn't any way to appeal?"

"No," said Béliard. "That, on the other hand, is not at all standard practice. But don't worry about it, don't take it badly. And besides, frankly, just between you and me, the park isn't always a picnic. You can definitely get bored at times. Of course, you've got the sun all the time, but I'm sure you'll agree that the best part of sunlight is the shade. There are even some who have a very hard time dealing with it at first, and then eventually they get used to it. Fact is, they don't really have a choice."

"Fine," said Max, "I'm willing to go along with the programme, but what exactly is this urban zone about?"

"Very simple," said Béliard. "People form all sorts of ideas about it, but you'll see it isn't so bad, either. In a nutshell, we're sending you back home, there you have it. Well, actually, when I say back home, I mean to Paris, you understand."

"Until when?" worried Max. "When does that part end?"

"That's all there is," said Béliard. "It will never end. It's rather how the system works, if you like. But if it makes you feel any better, remember that it never ends for those in the park, either." And as Max was about to console himself that returning home would at least allow him to find his loved ones again, see people again, resume normal activities, Béliard immediately intercepted his thought.

"There are only three basic rules in the urban zone," he specified. "First, it's forbidden to contact people you knew in life, forbidden to make yourself recognised, forbidden to renew contacts. But that," said Béliard with a knowing air, "shouldn't be a problem."

"And why is that?" Max wanted to know.

"We're going to modify some small aspects of your appearance," Béliard announced, "just some little things. But don't get upset, it's very subtle."

"But I don't want that!" Max protested vehemently. "I refuse."

"I told you not to get upset," said Béliard. "When we put you back together the other day, we already took care of a few details."

"What details?" panicked Max, running his hands over his face.

"You see?" said Béliard. "You didn't even notice. You're going to have a little more plastic surgery, nothing very complicated, just a few finishing touches, some minor touch-ups here and there, and after that no-one will be able to recognise you. As far as your appearance is concerned, we'll handle the entire thing. As I said, nothing too drastic. And let me reassure you straight away, it won't change very much for you. People can't imagine how peaceful it is to be incognito.

"The second point is that you also have to change identity, naturally. That will be your responsibility to take care of. You'll have to see about obtaining identity papers and such."

"Hold on a minute," Max objected plaintively, "give me a chance. I don't know anything about all that. I wouldn't have a clue how to go about it."

"That's not my problem," Béliard said harshly, with his former abruptness. But, seeing how lost Max looked, he ended up digging into his pocket and pulling out an address book, which he leafed through. "I could give you an address," he said, "but it's in South America, and I'm not even sure it's still valid. Still, I'll try to arrange a little excursion for you."

"But I don't know that part of the world," Max repeated. "I don't even know how to get there."

"We'll give you a hand at first," said Béliard, "but after that it'll be up to you to find your way. Right. The third rule, as I've already mentioned, is that it's forbidden to resume your old activity. In the broad sense, I mean. That includes any professional practice related to the one you used to have. You won't be able to play the artist as before, you understand, you'll have to hold down a real job like everyone else. You'll need to find something. But there again, you'll have a little help at first."

"And what about money?" asked Max.

"We've thought of that," answered Béliard. "We'll also give

you a little something to start off with. Well, I think I've covered everything. Your operation is scheduled in twenty minutes, and you'll be leaving immediately afterwards. I'll come back to fetch you in a while."

No sooner had he shut the door behind him than it opened again on Dino, whose smile was a notch below its habitual register. "So you'll be leaving us, sir," Dino said gravely.

"Yes," Max said in an anxious tone. "They're sending me back home. I don't really know what's going to happen."

"So I heard, sir. I'm sorry."

"Dino," Max suddenly thought, "could I get a little something to drink? I think I could use one right now."

"I'm afraid that would be difficult, sir," said the valet. "Your stay here is over. To tell the truth, I just came to prepare the room for the next occupant, you understand, they never stay empty for long. That's the problem with this job, the turnover is very fast and you never have much time to get to know people."

"I understand," said Max. "I understand."

Béliard reappeared just then, accompanied by the stretcher-bearer, and Max said a quick farewell to the valet. "Right, well, good-bye, Dino, thanks for everything and sorry to have bothered you."

"Bothered me, sir?" said Dino. "Come now, not in the slightest, never."

"Yes, I did," said Max. "You know, that question I asked you."

"Really, sir," went Dino, again displaying his classic smile, this time seasoned with an unaccustomed wink—a direct quote from a scene with Raquel Welch in the film *Bandolero!*, which explicitly answered the question.

"Come on, come on, let's go," said Béliard impatiently.

Back in the operating room, Max was offered no commentary by the surgeon, who in any case wasn't the one from the other day. Nor, to put him under, did they use an injection, as he expected: this time it was an anaesthetising mask, promptly clamped over his face, that once more plunged him into artificial slumber, without leaving him time to wonder where, when, how, or even if he would one day wake up again.

III

TWENTY

HE WAS AWAKENED by the chaotic bucking of a hydrofoil, a small yellow craft in the white of dawn slapping over a wide river the colour of glue. Opening his eyes, Max noticed, in the distance to his right, a city of respectable proportions and shabby appearance built near the water. "Iquitos," the pilot soberly announced—a young fellow with a pencil moustache, a face of ochre marble, and dark fake Ray-Bans treated with iridium.

Now immobile, the hydrofoil rocked gently on the surface of the waves, in the extreme heat already rising at that hour of the day. After a few minutes, the young fellow clicked a latch on the door, pointing with his chin to a motorised canoe that approached at top speed and then came to a halt next to the vehicle's floats. Max thanked the pilot with a wave of his hand before jumping on to the canoe, which immediately started up again towards the port terminal located upstream from the city. The canoe driver was as uncommunicative as the hydrofoil pilot, and

Max was carrying only a small bag of unknown origin, containing a few basic toiletries that he didn't recall having purchased. Nothing else, no change of clothes, just an envelope holding a small bundle in a local currency unfamiliar to him, along with a slip of paper bearing the address of a hotel and a telephone number preceded by the name "Jaime". This bundle might be enough to live on for a short while in a country with a weak exchange rate, which at first glance, from afar, the rather miserable aspect of the place suggested that it might be. Max didn't dare ask the canoe driver where exactly in South America they were; it might have sounded strange, and in any case Max spoke neither Spanish nor Portuguese. Whatever the case, he'd have to figure out how to buy something to wear, for at the moment he had on only a shirt, a pair of canvas trousers without a belt, and yellow shoes that pinched his feet.

Located to the north-west of the South American continent, at equal distance from three borders, squeezed between the tropical forest and the Amazon river, Iquitos is a city of 300,000 inhabitants built on the right bank of this considerable estuary. It was officially designated an Amazonian port by the sole clause of Law no. 14702 on January 5, 1964. Its average temperature is 36°. Surrounded by the river and several of its branches, Iquitos might also appear to be a kind of island, since no road leads there; the only way to reach it is by air or water. Along the bank is a series of small docks like the one they were approaching, at the far end of which sat a Ford occupied by two men named Oscar and Esau, who eventually extricated themselves from this vehicle to come and welcome Max.

Much younger than Esau, more talkative and plump, short-sleeved shirt and a gold chain around his neck, Oscar spoke excellent French. Without explicitly naming Béliard, he intimated that he was aware of his influence and the formalities Max needed to handle, before inviting him to get in the car. They turned on to the dilapidated road that must have led to the centre of town. Dark suit, tie, slicked-back hair, thick glasses with large frames, Esau contented himself with driving, silently and slowly, the dented old air-force-blue Ford. The seats and steering wheel of the car were covered in a yellowish plush, and a horizontal band along the bottom of the windscreen was covered by a protective runner of quilted red velour with gold fringes. As this unstable runner kept sliding from its support, falling at the slightest pothole, Esau spent most of his time patiently setting it back in place with one hand, his primary concern apparently being the maintenance of this object that Oscar sometimes helped readjust. Constantly distracted by his task, Esau drove at an average speed of twenty miles an hour, with a fair number of dips to about twelve. When for no apparent reason one of the two windscreen wipers spontaneously began working, scraping the heavily pocked windscreen with a raucous screech, Esau vainly tried every knob on the dashboard to switch it off before letting the matter drop. It was getting hotter and hotter in this car with no air conditioning, and as for the protective runner that continued to slip off, Esau let that drop, too.

In Iquitos, at the corner of Fitzcarrald and Putumayo, the room that they had reserved for Max on the second floor of the Hotel Copoazú was as elementary as could be, its window looking directly out on to a solid wall. Iron single bed; little hospital-style TV attached to the flimsy wall; plastic chair; a bedside table holding a lamp, a telephone, and the television remote control: nothing more. The bathroom was meagre, and Max put off as long as he could checking in the mirror to see what he looked like now. Lying on the bed, the back of his neck twisted by the flimsy pillow propped against the metal headboard, he skipped through some forty public and private channels of local, neighbouring, and North American origin. The three national stations broadcast election results, which Max, although he grasped very little of the language, seemed to understand were being contested. Still, he couldn't stop thinking about his face, with a mixture of fear and impatience, dreading what he desperately wanted to see.

He finally decided to have a shave, comb his hair, and brush his teeth as an excuse to get himself into the windowless bathroom. As the neon light above the mirror naturally didn't work, he could only view himself in silhouette, but from that perspective, at least, nothing appeared significantly different. He waited another long while in front of the television before calling the front desk to ask in his rudimentary English if someone could come and replace the bulb—*Please could you change the light in the bathroom, it doesn't work*—*Sí, señor*—which also took a fair amount of time.

Then, once the repair was made and Max was alone again, he took a deep breath before daring to go and look at himself.

Nice work. They hadn't made a mess of it. While Max was patently unrecognisable, you couldn't attribute his transformation to anything in particular. Not his nose, forehead, eyes, cheeks, mouth, or chin—nothing had changed. Everything was there. Rather, it was the arrangement of these features, the relationship between them, that had been imperceptibly altered, although Max himself couldn't have said exactly how, in what order or which direction. But the fact was, he wasn't the same any more—or rather, he was the same but incontestably someone else: his face might appear vaguely familiar to someone who had known him, but it would surely go no further than that. He tried opening his mouth wide to make sure they had left him his teeth: they had. He recognised his old fillings and his little crown, but there again an indefinable new maxillary order seemed to reign.

Perplexed, at once relieved and horrified, Max turned on the tap to give himself a glass of water. But on the one hand, he was trembling so hard that it took several attempts to fill the vile cup, and on the other the water from the tap, which under European climates has to pass sixty-two quality parameters to be deemed potable, must in Iquitos have had roughly a few dozen, at the most. So Max called down to the front desk again to ask for an *agua mineral* to be sent up. And while they were at it, considering that this kind of thing doesn't happen to you every day, judging moreover that after his week of relative abstinence at the Centre he certainly deserved one, why didn't they also bring him a bottle of pisco, with ice and some lemon. Sí, señor. While waiting, he went back to look at himself again in the mirror. He'd get used to it. He didn't have any choice, of course, but fine, he'd get used to it, maybe even quicker than he thought. He switched off the neon light, left the bathroom, and, just as he was turning up the sound on the television, someone knocked at his door.

It was the manager with his tray, holding everything Max had asked for. Once the manager had left, Max uncapped the bottle of pisco and eagerly poured himself a drink, but the taste of the alcohol was repulsive, vile, unbearably emetic, and Max had to run to spit it out in the sink. What's going on here? Very strange. And yet pisco is actually quite good. Whatever the case, after having washed and carefully wiped his glass, Max rinsed out his mouth with *agua mineral*, opened his bag, removed the envelope, opened the envelope, took out the piece of paper with the telephone number jotted on it, sat down on the bed, pulled the telephone towards him, and dialled the number.

TWENTY-ONE

AFTER HANGING UP the phone, Max left the hotel with his empty little bag, which he spent the afternoon filling by doing some shopping in the streets of Iquitos: clothing suited to the climate—light jacket and shirts, cotton trousers, pack of underwear; basic necessities, such as a belt, razor-blades, soap, and shampoo; as well as a larger bag to hold it all plus the folded smaller bag. Back at the hotel, he ate alone, the clink of his silverware producing sinister echoes in the empty restaurant dining room. Then he went upstairs and soon got into bed. He slept fitfully and, having risen early, decided to leave this establishment without further ado.

That morning, Max quickly found two rooms to let in the dilapidated mansion of a former rubber tycoon. The façade of this residence was covered with glazed ceramic tiles, beautifully decorated though now mostly cracked; *azulejos* that, in the days of his splendour and Iquitos's prosperity, the tycoon had had shipped from Portugal via fluvial and maritime routes, on the same ship that carried his dirty laundry each week to the Lisboan laundries. The barred windows looked directly out on the Amazon past Avenida Coronel Portillo and, from his room, Max could thus enjoy a view of the wooden houses built at river level, some floating, others on stilts. Large sea-going vessels passed by in the distance, motorbikes spluttered on the tarmacked avenue, birds circled above the traffic of the canoes, and small children played in the rubbish. Max absently surveyed this spectacle, daydreaming, developing his thoughts in two directions. First, he would have to get used to living with his new appearance, while waiting for the documents bearing his new identity that they would deliver in a few days at the airport cafeteria, as agreed the day before on the phone. Second, while his rent for the two rooms wasn't exorbitant, Max had nonetheless felt a twinge of worry when calculating the fraction it deducted from his little bundle. The identity forgers surely weren't in it for the good of the cause, and what he had left wouldn't take him very far. We'll wait and see.

Resigned to spending his money, he soon came across a place where he could take his meals: the Regal restaurant, located in an iron building on Plaza de Armas, above the British consulate. The iron had the drawback of amplifying the heat like a cymbal, but you could eat fish from the river while watching the girls who strolled across the square in tight, inaccessible groups and the men who gathered around the sewer drains, amusing themselves by fishing for rats with some line and a bit of omelette tied to the end. And here, as in every tropical restaurant in the world, you could see huge fans reflected in the concavity of the saucers, spoons, and ladles like gigantic insects or tiny helicopters. Max stared at all of this with an interested but detached eye, the eye of a man resuscitated, restored to the world and looking at this world as if through a pane of glass.

As he didn't speak to anyone and no-one spoke to him, his main activity consisted in systematically and thoroughly perusing the local and national press, which soon gave him an elementary grasp of Spanish. On the heels of an obviously fixed recount, the controversy over the electoral results still occupied the front pages in bold headlines, but Max was more interested in the back sections. Entirely photographic, these related in detail the social lives of the local and neighbouring ruling classes. Thus one could see, in the context of various inaugurations, receptions, premières, marriages, and cocktail parties, groups of personalities flashing wide smiles at the paparazzi with glasses in hand. Evening gowns, dinner jackets, champagne, and pisco sours, general gaiety, dizzying multiplicity of faces, none of which, of course, was familiar to him. Max, whose stay at the Centre had made him neither forget his cares nor lose his habits, continued to verify automatically if Rose might perchance figure in one of these photos. Naturally, such a hypothesis was highly improbable, but when you got down to it, having disappeared so completely, she could just as easily turn up married to an Argentine banker or a Guatemalan industrialist, or maybe a Paraguayan senator.

One can get used to Iquitos fairly quickly—more so than to those yellow shoes that Max still hadn't managed to replace. It's fairly easy to get around, and one finds oneself not too badly off. Apart from his money worries, which he kept putting off thinking about seriously, Max felt as if he was on holiday by the end of his third day. But that was the day of his meeting with the identity broker, at Francisco Secada Vigneta Airport, located two and a half miles from the centre of town. To get there, Max had to take one of those motocars whose drivers were constantly offering him their services. The motocar, a covered scooter with a seat in the back, is the Amazonian equivalent of the rickshaw, though lacking the side panels and with a slightly different body from its Indian counterpart. Unlike the latter, it is not spangled with political or pious transfers—just a tiger or two, at times, painted on the seat—and isn't equipped with a meter. But as we all know, a rickshaw meter isn't worth much. We all know just how unreliable it can be, and so the fare for a ride is debated from the start no less bitterly with a *motocarista* than with a Tabul rickshaw-wallah, a Beninese *zemidjian*, or a Laotian *túk-túk* driver. As for the comfort provided by each of these vehicles, it is more or less comparable in every case.

Arriving at the airport, Max had no difficulty finding the cafeteria nor, virtually alone in the middle of it, the aforementioned

Jaime to whom he'd spoken three days earlier on the telephone, sitting before a steaming double espresso. Jaime must have been about Max's age; the small, ironic spectacles of a presbyopic filtered his knowing gaze. Left arm in a cast buried under a sweater buried under a jacket buried under a coat buried under a scarf buried under a hat—but, despite the steamroom atmosphere, these superimpositions did not seem to bother him overmuch. No sooner had they started talking than an old shoe-shine boy, haggard and dressed in rags, came to squat at Max's feet and, without asking his permission, immediately began to polish his shoes, which Max let him do without overseeing the operation.

"Right," said Jaime, "everything is almost ready. All we need now is an ID photo. If we could have it by the day after tomorrow, the papers could be ready at the end of the week."

"Fine. And tell me," worried Max, "do you know exactly how much this is going to cost?"

"Hard to say just yet," Jaime eluded. "We haven't drawn up the final invoice."

Then, concerning the shoe-shine boy who had finished his task and was now standing, trembling lightly in silence and staring fixedly at him, Max asked the same question.

"And what about him? How much should I give him?"

"A one-sol coin will do," decreed Jaime.

Max paid the shoe-shine boy without looking at him and arranged a second rendezvous with the forger, who then walked away. Left alone, Max cast a glance at his shoes. For lack of yellow shoe polish, no doubt, Max's footwear had been made violet, a beautiful and spectacular violet. Maybe they really weren't any worse like that, but still. Max stood up and left the airport, staring at the new colour of his feet. Well, if one was going to change identity, might as well start from the ground up.

TWENTY-TWO

THE DAYS THAT FOLLOWED didn't go nearly so well. Time passed ever more slowly and Max grew ever more concerned about money. For whatever one might think, despite his stay at the Centre and the tragic event that had preceded it, his personal situation did not prevent him from experiencing the classic feelings and needs of the organism. Hunger, heat, thirst (even without pisco), the desire for elementary creature comforts—all this raises problems that only money can solve. The humblest lifestyle is still subject to a budget. But Max could see his resources dwindling visibly, inexorably.

Added to this was an increasing sense of isolation. While discovering Iquitos had initially been enough to occupy him without his needing to speak to anyone, by now Max had had enough of tourism; by now he couldn't stand the solitude of this godforsaken hole any more. No way to share a few words with anyone on Plaza de Armas, neither the pretty girls nor the rat fishermen.

And if he sometimes managed, in his budding Spanish, to chat a bit with natives, mainly the ageing waiters of the Regal, it was only to hear pessimistic and resigned news of the city: exploding suicide rate, omnipresence of religious cults, massive drug traffic, practice of black magic, and I'll spare you the rest. All this was pretty discouraging and didn't exactly inspire Max to try to settle here. He had bouts of depression, days of boredom, the kind of listless boredom engendered by the union of solitude and modest means. He sometimes lost all desire to walk around Iquitos, what's the point, and once he even spent the entire day shut up in his two rooms, pacing restlessly between them, a caged beast who only stopped now and then to contemplate, through the bars of his window, the river with its unchanging colours.

That day, to take his mind off things, Max decided to write to his sister, thereby breaking the strict regulations that Béliard had recited to him. He spent a good hour composing his letter, in which he explained everything, recounted everything, complained about everything, and even had the nerve in conclusion to ask Alice for money. But once he had signed, read, and folded his letter, slipped it into an envelope and licked the adhesive strip, the troubles began. First, Max cut his upper lip on the flap of the envelope—a wound that, although very fine and benign, proved to be disproportionately painful; second, the rancid fish taste of the glue spreading through his mouth was abominable; third, Max stopped to think about the problems he was courting if Béliard were to press an investigation, now that he'd left behind some compromising saliva—the Centre's doctors surely hadn't gone so far as to alter his DNA. And finally, reflecting on, fourth, the extreme distress Alice might feel on receiving it, Max opened the envelope, read his letter over one last time, then ripped it up and burned the pieces.

At the Tropical Paradise Lodge on Putumayo Boulevard, where he had gone to nick a few leaflets for reading matter, he was offered the opportunity to take his mind off things by enjoying a canoe ride down the river. It would be another expense, of course, but what the hell, the half-day was still within his means. From several angles, the dark blocks of the Amazonian forest some-times called to mind certain areas of the park he'd visited with Béliard. Infested with mosquitoes, the waterways were lined with trees that grew following a bizarre logic, as if prey to a hereditary insanity, which went no small way towards fostering a sense of unease. They came across other canoes, rowed by silent locals transporting crates, bags, rubbish bins, or chickens in cages. They saw dogs, and once a fat iguana on a protruding branch, or more precisely a fat, female, pregnant, flabby iguana, which the canoe driver tried to capture to steal her egg—nothing tastier, the man assured him, than soft-boiled iguana egg.

On the appointed day, Max took another motocar back to the airport. Jaime was there, again swaddled in the convection-oven temperature, this time sitting in front of a hot chocolate. He handed Max a small bag made of embroidered cotton—local craftsmanship, handmade, he pointed out, a gift—containing the perfect copy of a French passport in the name of Salvador, Paul André Marie, French nationality, born on the same day as Max with Max's photo beneath, accompanied by no children on page four and authentic French fiscal stamps on page five. On page seven, in the first empty space reserved for visas, there was even a stamp attesting to his arrival in the country's capital, several weeks earlier, at Jorge Chávez International airport. It all looked impeccable.

While Max leafed through this object, Jaime withdrew from his pocket and handed him a folded sheet of paper on which a long number was inscribed. This number, the amount of the invoice for the passport, corresponded precisely, down to the last centavo, to what Max was carrying that very moment in the pockets of his new trousers: apparently they had kept close tabs on him, watched over his slightest expenditures, meticulously calculated what he had left, and now Max was utterly broke. As this must have shown on his face: "What's the matter?" said Jaime. "Is something wrong?" Max didn't have time to answer before the other, smiling as if he had been waiting only for this, was already making him a proposition so classic and devoid of imagination that it's embarrassing to report it. It would involve, as is only too common in this sort of caper, transporting a certain something abroad—to France, as it happened—for a certain remuneration. The situation is so common that there isn't even any need to specify the nature of this something, enclosed in a lizard-skin valise with locked, gilded-metal clasps, that Jaime, bending down, pulled out from under the table and placed on top.

"Here, this is all you'll have to carry," he explained. "It's nothing. Discreet, easy work, and paid. Not in local currency, trust me on that. You'll get dollars, the freshest bills around."

"Sure," said Max, "I don't mind, but when would I be going?"

"Right away," answered Jaime. "Your plane leaves in forty-five minutes."

"And what about my things?" worried Max.

"No problem," said Jaime, bending down once more, "I've got them right here. They stopped by your place to pick them up after you left." He handed over the belongings, carefully folded in their bag, and here are your tickets and here's your money. Max took a moment to count this money: dollars indeed, but very few of them, barely enough to last two or three days in Iquitos, in other words two or three hours in France. But for now, what else could he do?

"Right," said Max. "Fine."

TWENTY-THREE

MAX, HIS SUITCASE, and his bag did not have long to wait: immediate boarding. In the lounge at Iquitos airport, locals departing for Lima crossed paths with clusters of holiday-makers come to tread the limbo of the Amazonian forest, study the natives, consult their shamans, and have their minds exploded by the ingestion of *ayahuasca*. The luggage of both groups was carefully and suspiciously sniffed by two dogs kept on a leash and muzzled, whose absence of reaction at the passage of the lizard-skin suitcase at least allowed for the hope that it didn't contain any narcotics. Then, as soon as Max was seated in the small plane it began moving at top speed, attaining its altitude and cruising velocity in the blink of an eyelid, attesting to the professionalism of the pilots. This country, in fact, maintains a long tradition of virtuoso aviators, taking off at the appointed time and landing at the exact moment without getting bogged down in considerations or niceties—never hesitating to dive towards their goal, for instance, almost on a vertical trajectory and ignoring the stages of decompression entirely, heedless of the passengers who clap their hands in unison over their eardrums and howl in pain.

On the other hand, Max had a longer wait in Lima, where he passed the time reading through the newspapers, pleased to note his dazzling progress in Spanish, but anxious about what awaited him in Paris. Then, once on board, he dispensed with the mimo-drama of safety precautions performed by the stewardesses, who then distributed among the passengers orange juice and sweets, blankets, and headphones featuring various musical programmes. A knob embedded in the armrests allowed one to choose among these programmes: selections of easy listening, jazz, ethnic, and classical music. As the aeroplane began to taxi, Max put on his headphones to have something to do, automatically stopping at the classical selection where he immediately identified an *Impromptu* by Schubert in midstream, the Allegro in E-flat from Op. 90. But no sooner had he recognised the work than he also recognised his own performance, recorded five years earlier at Cerumen. He pretended not to notice, the way one feigns not to see a bothersome acquaintance in the street, except that this time the acquaintance was himself. He immediately changed programmes, then finally gave up; in any case the headphones were hurting his ears like an ill-fitted prosthesis. Max preferred listening to the sound of the Boeing engines, which was deep and penetrating, fundamental like an endless breath, not like those little Airbus motors that give off the sound of an old cultivator. Then he eventually fell asleep.

It was raining hard in Paris when the aeroplane touched down at Roissy-Charles-de-Gaulle, the kind of heavy rain that seems to fall from very high up and that Max had noticed, several days earlier, from the windows of the Centre. After customs, where, nothing to declare, no-one bothered to inspect the contents of his bag and suitcase, he passed through the doorway to the main hall unimpeded. There, facing the flow of arrivals, several individuals seemed to be waiting: two wives equipped with children ready to throw their arms around the first available neck, three unknown persons holding cardboard signs with names on them. Max did not immediately react when he spotted, on one of them, his new identity written in capitals; then, remembering, he walked straight up to it.

The unknown person holding it was absurdly wearing a beard, hat, dark glasses, and a raincoat buttoned to his Adam's apple. Still brandishing a card with Max's name even as he watched him approach, he dangled at the end of his other arm a suitcase of moderate size that he immediately held out to Max, without, for lack of available prehensile organ, shaking his hand.

"I'm Schmidt," he said, "and here are your belongings. I trust you have the suitcase."

"Here," said Max, handing it over.

"Good," said Schmidt, taking it. "Let's go and get a taxi."

A fairly short queue at the taxi rank, after which the so-called Schmidt gave the driver an address, an odd number on Boulevard Magenta. Max discreetly studied this improbable Schmidt, with his exaggerated surplus of anonymity attributes—although in truth, he wasn't certain they were really artifices; all of it could have been entirely normal for him. Then, deciding to cut short his contemplation—Schmidt probably didn't much appreciate people looking at him—Max turned in the other direction to ponder the landscape. It felt as if he was coming home after a very long absence, even though his combined stays at the Centre and in Iquitos had probably lasted no more than two weeks, but under the circumstances it was understandable to think that way. Through the taxi window, he saw the flat low-rise buildings and tall towers of the eastern suburbs that are visible around Bagnolet, when you return from the airport on the A3 motorway. Max had always found it hard to believe that these buildings contained real flats housing real people, with real kitchens and real bathrooms, real bedrooms where they authentically coupled, actually reproduced—it was scarcely imaginable.

But as it happened, the lodgings selected for him by the services of the Centre would be hardly more desirable. Schmidt, after remaining silent on the motorway, specified the route to follow once they hit the peripheral boulevard and, on Boulevard Magenta, halfway between Place de la République and Gare de l'Est, the taxi pulled up at an hotel. While not exactly luxurious, this establishment, named the Montmorency, wasn't quite a flea-pit, either. It possessed a foyer, two conference rooms, and a bar. They didn't take the lift: without stopping at the front desk, where a shapeless receptionist was marking time, Schmidt immediately beckoned to Max to follow him up a steep staircase that did not appear to have been built for the use of the clientele. On the uppermost floor, two rows of brown doors, opposite each other and very closely spaced, filed down a dark yellow corridor. Schmidt pulled a key from his pocket and the fourth door on the right opened on to a narrow room, wall-papered with faded flowers and fitted with flimsy furniture apart from an overly large bed, with a washbasin as its sole sanitary facility.

"Here you are," said Schmidt, "this is your home. There's a shower and a toilet on the landing."

Max walked up to the French window, pulled back the curtains, whose metal rings squeaked on the metal rod, and opened it on to the tumult of the boulevard that immediately began roaring and bounding into the cramped space.

"One problem," Max reminded him, immediately closing the window. "I have practically no money."

"The first month's rent is taken care of," Schmidt indicated. "After that, it'll be up to you to pay out of your salary."

"Salary," Max repeated uncomprehendingly.

"Of course salary," the other confirmed. "You've been assigned to the bar. I'll show you."

They therefore went down to the cellar of the establishment. As the bar was empty at that hour of the morning, Schmidt introduced him to his future work area, the multicoloured collection of bottles, the glasses of all sizes, the utensils, saucers, cocktail shakers, strainers, juice extractors, and spice racks. On a hanger in the cupboard hung a worn red jacket; a gilded metal rectangle was already pinned to its lapel with the name Paul S. engraved on it.

"Here you are," said Schmidt, "your work uniform. You have two days to get over jet lag, and on Monday you start. The management knows the story, if there are any problems you take it up with them. We will surely not have occasion to meet again . . . good luck."

Back in his room, Max pulled from his bag the items he had bought in Iquitos: garments that were too exotic and lightweight for the climate here, still impregnated with tropical aromas that he breathed in nostalgically before putting them away in the narrow white melamine armoire. Then he opened the suitcase that Schmidt had given him. It contained a dark grey suit, a pair of black trousers, two white shirts, a black tie, and three pairs of Y-fronts, as well as a pair of black shoes wrapped in a newspaper from the day before. All these clothes, of synthetic fabric, approximate size, and mediocre quality, seemed to have been worn by countless others before being put through numerous industrial washes. Welcome to the urban zone.

TWENTY-FOUR

MAX SPENT HIS TWO DAYS OFF walking around Paris. First he tried a few experiments in his old neighbourhood of Château-Rouge, as a way of verifying the effect produced by the plastic surgeons' work. He went incognito to see the shopkeepers he had habitually frequented, whom he used to call by name, and who for their part had ended up, despite his not exactly sociable nature, considering him a nominal regular. He observed their reactions when he entered their shops, making a few small purchases—a pack of Kleenex here, the evening paper there—looking them in the eye more and more intently, but without the others ever showing the slightest sign of recognition.

It even happened on the first day that, as he was leaving his ex-pharmacy, he ran smack into the woman with the dog, flanked by the latter to her left and her husband to her right. It was the first time Max had seen the three of them together; they looked rather content to be that way but showed no reaction when they crossed his path: they even met his gaze for a few seconds, then walked off as if he didn't exist. Only the dog, after a brief latency period, turned back towards Max with a perplexed expression, braking for an instant and knitting his brow—that odour reminds me of something, confound it, I've already sniffed that somewhere, but where? To give himself time to study the question in depth, the animal even stopped to piss lengthily against the right rear tyre of a Fiat Panda while examining Max, who for his part, wanting to verify once more the transformation of his appearance, leaned discreetly and symmetrically towards the vehicle's left rearview mirror. Then, yanked by his leash, the dog seemed to drop the matter, letting his attention drift toward a band of soaked, hirsute, rumpled pigeons who—the proof that they're aware of their filth—had come to take a lustral bath in a gutter of flowing water before flying heavily off again.

Since he was in the neighbourhood, Max decided to brave it still further by going to see his sister. He would just try to get a look at her, without making contact, merely to reassure himself that she was all right. He would proceed carefully, without exposing himself to Alice's view, for, despite the know-how of the Centre specialists and given what had just happened with the dog, it wasn't far-fetched to think that his own sister—blood thicker than water, etc.—would recognise who he was. Accordingly, he took up a position not far from the entrance to his building, inanely hidden behind a newspaper; and in fact, after an hour or two of waiting, he saw Alice come out, stop in front of the doorway, and look at her watch. And then, surprise surprise, here was Parisy emerging from the building in turn to come and join her and take her arm. Parisy's bearing, a slight nonchalance in his suit along with something lighter, more familiar, in his behaviour, suggested that the impresario had finally made it with Max's sister, perhaps had moved in with her, and perhaps had, troubling perspective, even taken over Max's studio. It nonetheless seemed to Max, from a distance, that Alice was speaking a bit harshly to Parisy, who answered while waving his other arm in agitation—in short, it seemed as if they were already fighting. Max watched them walk away, not following them, then set off again. He continued to look at all the people he came across in the street, wondering about each one's status: maybe there were others like him, who had passed through the Centre before coming back here; maybe there were many of them; maybe, when you got down to it, they were even in the majority.

Once his two days of recuperation were over, Max, as scheduled, began his new vesperal service as a bartender. It turned out that the bar was not only empty in the morning; it was that way almost all the time. Not empty enough, however, for Max to take it entirely easy: there was always, at some advanced hour of the evening, one customer or other, sometimes alone but much more often accompanied by a woman. And Max, noticing that it was usually the same woman but not the same customer, and that their brief stays at the bar (whispered confabulations in which numbers played a part) most often concluded with the ordering of two drinks or a bottle to be brought to a room, soon understood what was what. So there weren't a lot of people there to pass the time with, which didn't keep him from being asked now and again for atypical cocktails that were a real bore to make. Alcohol itself was no longer something to pass the time with: it seemed that, since his attempted pisco in Iquitos, Max's appetite for it had curiously evaporated.

And every night at around 1.30 a.m., he returned to his room after having done the till and wiped down the bar. He took off his red jacket and the rest and immediately went to bed, reviewing his cocktail recipes in a special book and taking pains to memorise them. Then he had trouble falling asleep in his large bed, for large beds, let's not forget, are made for two people to find each other in beneath the sheets, and these sheets themselves are designed to be folded by a couple. Just see how a man trying to fold his large sheet alone soon ends up in an awkward position, entangled in himself as much as in the sheet; see how his short arms struggle to attain the required breadth. Whereas a couple, folding the sheet together while talking about other things, have it much easier—not to mention the additional interest, the intimate strategy, of anticipating, on either side of the dividing sheet, which direction the other will turn it in so as to harmonise with his or her movement.

But then see, too, how things work out. After several painful weeks of solitude in the depths of his red jacket, Max ended up meeting someone. As often happens in life, this would occur at his place of work, at the hotel itself. The receptionist. Not at all as shapeless as he had originally thought. She was, on the contrary, a tall reddish-blonde, not fantastically wonderful-looking, but not too bad, always dressed fairly sexily, with high heels up to there. He might have noticed her earlier, but the truth is, during his first days at the Hotel Montmorency, Max hadn't noticed anything at all, not even that it was raining all the time.

Now one day, when the sky was promising enough to clear up, Max ran into the receptionist not far from the hotel, right in the street, lit by a shaft of gentle sunlight. She was with a small boy in the four-five range who was complaining in an anxious voice that something black kept following him, that something was there and it didn't want to go away. "It's just your shadow, darling," the young woman explained. "It's nothing. Well, it's not nothing, but it's just your shadow." That sentence persuaded Max, who felt pretty shadowy himself, to take an interest in this young lady. He would proceed gradually. He had time.

He had time, but things nonetheless went faster than expected. One Wednesday Max suggested they go for coffee—O.K. Bought her some flowers—very O.K. Then invited her to dinner, next Sunday when he wasn't on duty at the bar—all the more O.K. in that the receptionist's son would be spending the night at his grandma's. Risked complimenting her overtly—absolutely O.K., and Max, as it happened, neither restrained nor recognised himself: you're so feminine, he told her, tracing rounded figures in the air, you're the very definition of feminine. To which she responded with a very pretty laugh. She was a single mother named Félicienne. What a beautiful name, Max enthused. And how well it suits you. So well, in fact, that their evening ended in a hotel, neither very far nor very different from the Montmorency.

TWENTY-FIVE

THEN, after his shift the next evening, Max went to see Félicienne at her place, and on the nights that followed he would no longer sleep much in his room at the hotel. The receptionist lived in a three-room apartment, hardly bigger than Bernie's on Rue Murillo: a living room and two bedrooms, the larger one being occupied by the kid, whose IQ they hadn't gauged yet and who answered, or didn't, depending on his mood, to the name of William—though in general, they just called him the kid.

At first, Max spent only his nights at Félicienne's, joining her after having closed his register and changed jackets, but always escaping from her place the moment he woke up. After breakfast in a nearby café, he would go back to the hotel to take a shower, then set off again to walk around Paris, sometimes stopping in a cinema—better to see a film than to watch the time pass on the ceiling of his inhospitable room, stretched out on his bed as if dead. But little by little Félicienne persuaded him to have breakfast with her, use the bathroom after her, accompany her to the babysitter's to drop off the kid, then escort her to the Montmorency. Not quite to the entrance: no sense in the whole staff knowing about them. They usually separated one street beforehand.

That was in the first stage, for it happened that things moved quickly—very, then too quickly. Max soon found himself being given a copy of the door key, along with a shelf in the cupboard for his change of clothes, which would rapidly land in the laundry basket next to the washing machine, after which, since according to Félicienne Max had nothing to do all day long, he saw himself being handed the iron. Responsibility for this iron was soon followed by the bestowing of shopping lists, on which figured a fleet of cleaning products whose directions Félicienne taught him to read and then apply, having already introduced him to the mop and broom cupboard, which would keep him busy until it was time to go and collect the kid from the babysitter's. From that point on, Max went to the cinema less often, now spending the free time he had left after shopping and cleaning in front of Félicienne's video, taking advantage of her subscription to a video club.

This evolution is hardly enviable, but then again, since things were going well with Félicienne sexually, this shared life was basically as good as any other. For lack of other alternatives, at least there was this. And so the time passed. Having finished his shift, Max joined Félicienne who was asleep, who on awakening gave him a little love before setting off to the hotel to receive the customers and answer the phone, leaving Max, sorry, leaving Paul to take care of the housework, and returning home just as he was setting off in turn to put on his red jacket and concoct spritzers, bronxes, manhattans, and flips for a clientele that, truth be told, was rapidly deteriorating. Plainly put, the vague provincial businessmen who took advantage of their brief stay in Paris to buy themselves a girl for the night were being replaced by a growing population of locals who fancied that kind of girl, and who often weren't even guests of the hotel; in short, there were more and more whores, often the same ones and often quite nice. Max wasn't offended—on the contrary—by this shift in population, which paid less attention to the dosage and quality of the cocktails that he still had some trouble mixing by the book.

Given their work conditions, Félicienne and Max hardly saw each other any more, except on Sundays when they took the kid out for some air—which kid, initially shy with Max, ended up letting himself be won over to the point of becoming very familiar, then more and more familiar, and soon much too familiar for Max's taste. They went to the Champ-de-Mars on Sundays, they went to Les Halles, to the park, they went for a walk down the Champs-Élysées. It always gave Max a funny feeling when Félicienne suggested Parc Monceau. He no longer dreaded the statue of Gounod next to the drinking fountain, nor even the one of Chopin not far from the children's playground, where the kid constantly stamped his feet to have yet another turn on whatever it was.

Nonetheless, Max began to feel bored. While he'd grown accustomed fairly quickly to his new physical appearance, strangely enough he had much more trouble with being called Paul, but perhaps someday he'd get used to that as well. And so time passed as if in a waiting-room, with a sense of leafing through magazines as worn-out, faded, and mind-numbing as Félicienne herself. On top of which, what did he really know about Félicienne, other than that she dwelled on insane claims about the past, bitterly insisting that in her youth she'd had measurements to kill for, a gift for languages, and perfect pitch? But, raised in modest surroundings, she'd had to enter working life early, thereby sacrificing a triple career as a world-famous top model, international interpreter, and renowned concert performer, having been forced to abandon the piano. Max, slicing the Sunday roast, masked with his indifference the intense relief produced by this third piece of information.

Indifference, yes, they would reach that point. Soon the arrangement with Félicienne would no longer be working so well. It's just that love—well, when I say love, I'm not sure it's the right word—is not only evanescent, but soluble. Soluble in time, money, alcohol, daily life, and a host of other things besides. Sexually, for example, it was not going well at all, Félicienne refusing his advances more and more often. In fact it was going so badly that Max, often, dreamily played a record he'd found one day at a discount shop near the Porte Saint-Denis, *The Best of Peggy Lee*, about which Félicienne, demonstrating a real hostility as if she suspected something, would sourly ask him how he could waste his time listening to that shit.

"No, no," said Max, "no reason. I just like it."

Nor did it help matters that he found it harder and harder to stand the kid, who, technologically very precocious, demanded the video-recorder for his own exclusive use, depriving Max of being able to watch one of the two videos with Dean Martin— his all-time greatest roles, in *Some Came Running* and *Rio Bravo*— purchased that same day at the same discount shop.

Several increasingly lack-lustre weeks flowed by like this until one night when, in the bar, while turning over and over the different ways of putting an end to this business with Félicienne, Max was artlessly preparing an alexandra—the composition of which is not all that complicated: three equal parts cognac, whipped cream, and crème de cacao. As he was struggling with the whipped cream, which was too firm after a prolonged stay in the fridge, he saw a man come in at the far end of the room, fairly short in stature and flanked by an immense redhead dressed in almost nothing.

Max knew the redhead a little, one of the new regulars he liked well enough, a sweet girl who ran on whisky-fizz, which is a refreshing drink served directly in a tumbler, very simple to prepare. Too absorbed in his task, he paid no attention to her new admirer, who sat down with her at a little table in the back, then, standing up again after a few seconds, started walking towards

Max, no doubt to impart what he wanted to drink. Now, Max had better things to do at that moment than to take an order, having just spilled all the whipped cream into the shaker, and, head down, he was just about to rebuff the outsider, when: "Monsieur Max?" uttered the outsider.

TWENTY-SIX

MAX JUMPED, sending the whipped cream spewing even further and raising his eyes to the outsider. Bernie.

"Monsieur Max," Bernie repeated with delight. "What are you doing here?"

"It's a long story," said Max, wiping a spurt of cream from his sleeve. "But how did you recognise me?"

Bernie didn't seem to understand the question. "Well, it's you," he said. "Why?" (One's true friends, Max melted inside.) "I'm really happy to see you," declared Bernie. "I've often wondered what became of you."

As he didn't seem to know about any of it, Max avoided going into the matter. "And how about you?" he asked. "What have you been up to?"

"I had some problems with Parisy," answered Bernie, "didn't he tell you? I got fed up, you see, he wasn't true to his word, and I left right after your concert at Gaveau, do you remember? I haven't seen him since."

"Of course," eluded Max, understanding that Bernie, who still maintained he never read the papers, must not have heard about what had happened to him, neither his disappearance nor, of course, the rest.

"But I immediately found something much better," Bernie continued. "I'm in show business now. I've completely broken with the classical crowd. I organise shows. Well, not exactly—I'm a concert promoter, if you like, and it's going pretty well. Ah, I never would have expected to find you here."

"Yes," said Max, "I needed to get away from what I was doing before, you understand, the milieu and all that. I needed a break myself."

"Right, right," Bernie said dubiously. "So you're happy here?"

"Not really," said Max, "but it's just for now. It's temporary."

"Even so, a man of your stature," lamented Bernie, "ending up here. I've never been to this place, but it doesn't strike me as all that great. I was just coming in for a drink with my friend."

"Of course," said Max, with a wide smile for the friend, which caused Bernie to glance down at his shoes.

"Listen," he said timidly, "if you ever wanted to make a change, I might be able to help."

"You think?" Max pretended to wonder with a detached air.

"Oh, definitely," said Bernie. "I'm sure I could find you something. Are you still playing the piano?"

"Well, actually, that's a bit complicated," said Max. "But anyway, what can I get you in the meantime?"

"It's mostly cocktails here, right?" said Bernie.

"Alas," admitted Max.

"Well, in that case, I'll have a rainbow," Bernie stated. "Hold on a minute, I'll ask my friend what she's drinking."

"Don't bother," said Max. "I think I know."

When Bernie returned the next day, alone, Max was wiping his tumblers while casting distracted glances at the two or three girls settled in that evening with their clients. While he was relieved that someone had finally recognised him, he was also a bit concerned about flouting Béliard's instructions. But after all, he himself hadn't done anything; it was Bernie who had recognised him, Bernie who had acted on his own, Bernie who was coming back to see him. It was also Bernie who had looked into things: an acquaintance of his named Gilbert had just opened an establishment off Rue d'Alésia.

"Very up-market," stressed Bernie, with a gesture towards the girls. "Not at all like here. Kind of a nightclub, very distinguished, very quiet, and they're looking for a pianist. What do you say?"

"In principle, I really shouldn't," said Max, "but what the hell." Yes, what the hell, what would the staff of the Centre know? Of course, it would again mean working in a bar—which, given

Max's past, bordered on just retribution, or repetition compulsion—but it was perhaps, and particularly, a welcome chance to rid himself of Félicienne. Although he didn't quite know how to go about it, as he explained in detail to his former bodyguard. "I tell you, Bernie, I can't take any more of that woman. And I don't have the first clue how to get away from her."

"Nothing could be simpler, Monsieur Max. Here's what we'll do."

TWENTY-SEVEN

AND THE FOLLOWING SUNDAY, after they had walked the kid, Max announced to Félicienne that he was taking her out to dinner that very evening, which would give him an opportunity to introduce her to an old friend of his.

They met in front of a large seafood restaurant on Place de l'Odéon. Bernie was already waiting, very elegant, standing very straight in a chic black unstructured suit, nothing like the outfits Max was used to seeing him in. Max only had the sordid grey suit left by Schmidt to wear; a striped tie bought by Félicienne failed to raise its sartorial level. From the moment they went in, the staff treated them with an attentiveness that rivalled the restaurant in the Centre. Félicienne, impressed by the setting and Bernie's elegance, tried not to show it. As she went to powder her nose before they were shown to their table, Max briefly took Bernie aside.

"There's just one thing I forgot to mention," he said.

"Yes, Monsieur Max?" said Bernie.

"Listen carefully, tonight you don't call me that, O.K.? Just call me Paul. I'll explain later."

"That's fine with me," said Bernie. "It's my stepson's name. It'll be easy to remember."

It must be obvious by now that Max is not exactly the world's jolliest fellow, the most relaxed or talkative person around, but as soon as they sat down at their table, he became someone else. Maintaining a smile that was by turns affectionate, complicit, seductive, kind, relaxed, and generous, he took the floor from the start and did not let it go, segueing gracefully between myriad anecdotes and light pleasantries, attentions and compliments, bons mots and witticisms, subtle observations and rare quotations, imaginary memories and historical comparisons, without ever getting bogged down or seeming as if he was hogging the spotlight. Bernie was convulsed with laughter at the slightest remark from Max, while Félicienne, dazzled, looked at him with a new tenderness and wide, emotion-filled eyes.

From aperitif to dessert, Max thus staged a spectacular performance. Hanging on his every syllable, Félicienne and Bernie smiled and laughed non-stop, she turning several times to Bernie to take this charming friend of Paul's as witness to her happiness, Paul's charming friend sometimes laying a discreet hand on Félicienne's shoulder to punctuate his hilarity. At times both of them looked at each other, delighted like enthusiastic spectators sitting in adjacent seats thanks to the luck of the draw of their tickets, who spontaneously, without knowing each other, connect in their enchantment. Charming ambiance, delectable evening. From the diners sitting around them to the waiters themselves, the whole room cast seduced, almost envious glances at this trio led by a Max in excellent form.

When suddenly, at the turn of a phrase, he immobilised both the fork above his plate and his smile, freeze-frame on the image, his gaze fixed on Félicienne and Bernie in a glacial stare. Disconcerted silence around the table.

"No, really, both of you," he said in a changed voice, "you think I haven't noticed your little game? You seriously believe I don't see what you're up to? You somehow imagine I'm going to put up with this right under my nose?"

And, standing up, Max pulled from his inside pocket a wad of notes that he dropped on the table before taking his leave for ever, without another word, wearing a bitter expression of wounded pride.

And the next morning, he met Bernie in a café near Châtelet.

"So," said Max, "how was I?"

"Excellent, Monsieur Max," said Bernie. "You were perfect."

"I owe it all to you, you know," said Max. "It was your idea. How did she take it?"

"The poor woman," said Bernie. "She didn't know what hit her. She needed consoling, so I took it upon myself. I saw her home and then, you know how it is."

"Very good," said Max, "you did well."

"So there you have it," said Bernie. "I'm seeing her again on Thursday."

"Just be careful," Max warned. "She's not exactly an easy customer."

"Oh," said Bernie, "I'm used to that. But now where are you going to live?"

"I don't want to go back to the hotel," Max indicated.

"No problem," said Bernie, "you can just come and stay at my place."

"I've been to your place," Max recalled. "It's too small."

"I've moved since," said Bernie. "Now I live on Boulevard du Temple. It's not as fashionable as Monceau, but I have a lot more room. I have the income for it now—you saw my suit last night, didn't you?"

"Speaking of which," said Max, "I owe you for dinner."

"Oh, don't worry about it, Monsieur Max," said Bernie. "We'll deal with that later. In the meantime, let's go and see Gilbert."

The establishment that Gilbert had recently opened was large, dark, and silent at this hour, as was Gilbert himself at all hours. The decor was elegant, sober, and distinguished, as Gilbert turned out to be as well.

"So you're a pianist," he said.

"Gosh," Max qualified, "let's say I used to be."

"Monsieur Max is a great artist," Bernie testified, his eyes bulging.

"You see," said Gilbert, "the fact is, I need someone reliable. I know all about the problems you can have with musicians. Would you mind submitting to a small audition?"

"Really, Gilbert," Bernie said indignantly, "you can't just insult him like that. You forget you're dealing with an artist of international stature."

"No problem," said Max, "as you wish. What would you like to hear? Classical or piano bar—whatever you prefer."

As Gilbert left the choice up to him, he performed "Laura", "Liza", "Celia", one after another, followed by one or two polonaises.

"That should do perfectly," judged Gilbert, but just at that moment the door to the establishment flew open and, visibly furious, Béliard made his appearance.

TWENTY-EIGHT

WITHOUT A WORD OF GREETING, without a glance at Gilbert or Bernie, Béliard walked straight up to Max with a determined step.

"What did I tell you?" he began, screaming. "If you think we're not watching, you've got another think coming. What you're doing here is a double violation, it's not right, it's a double infraction of the rules. Not only did you let yourself be recognised—"

"You can't blame me for that," Max interrupted him, pointing to Bernie. "*He* recognised *me*. It's your doctors' fault for not doing their job properly."

"Maybe so," shouted Béliard, "but then on top of it you're practising your former profession."

"Not in the slightest," pleaded Max, pointing to the piano. "I was just showing these gentlemen what I can do."

"Fine," said Béliard, calming down a bit too quickly, "I'll let you off this time."

He had changed since the Centre. He no longer displayed the

haughty, distant, and condescending composure that had antago-
nised Max from their first meeting. He now seemed hyper-tense,
taut with emotion, flying off the handle just as quickly as he'd
then let the matter drop. Gilbert and Bernie chose to move away
from the piano, sidling over towards a back room.

"Let's get out of here," Béliard decided, nodding his head in
their direction. "We'll be able to talk more freely outside."

They went out. The street. The cars passing by. The various
kinds of music escaping through the lowered windows of the
cars. Sometimes it was just rhythmic blips, sometimes heavy bass
lines that sent a shiver up the spine. At first they walked without
saying anything; then Béliard resumed speaking.

"I've come to put things back in order," he stated calmly. "So
now you're going to do me the favour of going back to your job at
the bar, all right? At the hotel where you've been assigned."

"Absolutely not," Max declared in a firm voice. "I don't ever
want to go back to that bar. I don't think I've done anything to
deserve that."

"You're beginning to get on my nerves, Delmarc," Béliard
started shouting again. "You're making my life very difficult.
You're not a very easy fellow to deal with, do you know that?"

"First of all, what are you doing here?" asked Max. "I thought
you always stayed at the Centre."

"They reassigned me," said Béliard. "I've been rather tired
lately. And anyway, as I said, I needed to deal with you. I'm going
to stay here a few days, long enough to put you back on the

straight and narrow. And besides, I have another, more important problem to take care of. I've got someone who escaped from the park—you remember the park?—who I have to bring back. It's work, it's really a lot of work."

"First you should get some rest," Max pointed out. "What hotel are you staying at?"

"I don't know," said Béliard, ready to collapse, "I just got here, I haven't had time to deal with it. Do you know of one?"

Advising him against the Montmorency, Max recommended the Holiday Inn on Place de la République. "It's not bad," he emphasised, "it's comfortable and centrally located. And on top of which, I've got a friend who's offered to put me up on Boulevard du Temple, which is just a stone's throw from République. We won't be far from each other, we can get together whenever you like."

"Maybe," said Béliard, letting his shoulders sag, "I don't know. I'm exhausted. Yeah, maybe that's what I'll do. Is République far from here?"

"A bit," said Max. "You'll be better off taking a taxi."

"Fine," said Béliard. "All right." Then, pulling himself together and wagging his finger: "But don't get any ideas about acting like a bloody fool behind my back, all right?"

"No acting like a bloody fool," said Max. "Go and get yourself settled. You get settled in, get some rest, and I'll call you in the morning, all right?"

"All right," said Béliard. "That's what we'll do."

Max hailed a taxi into which the other man jumped without

another word and which Max watched drive away. The fact is, Béliard seemed utterly depressed.

"It was nothing," said Max once back at Gilbert's, "just a friend who's going through a bad patch. Anyway, where were we? Shall I play you something else?"

"That won't be necessary," said Gilbert. "I thought you were very good."

"Right," said Max, "so when do I start?"

"How about Monday?" suggested Gilbert.

"Ah, I'm so happy," Bernie exclaimed ten minutes later, in another taxi that was carrying them towards Boulevard du Temple. "Monsieur Max, I'm proud of you."

"I should be thanking *you*," said Max. "Furthermore, you can call me just plain Max from now on. Or Paul. Whichever you like."

Bernie's new flat, at number 42, was indeed roomier than the one on Rue Murillo but also much noisier, as it looked directly on to the boulevard. Since the stepson's room was still unoccupied—"He's in Switzerland now," explained Bernie. "A big private school in Switzerland. He just keeps getting smarter and smarter"—Max moved into it without bothering to fetch his things from the hotel. An advance from Gilbert would allow him to buy all new clothes as of tomorrow, after he had met Béliard as arranged.

Béliard was decidedly less agitated than the day before. "I slept well," he informed Max. "I got some rest. I needed it." Without

Max having to plead his case, he made no more fuss about the new employment at Gilbert's. "I admit that business with the Montmorency was a bit harsh," he judged. "Basically, you can do as you wish, I'll smooth things over with Schmidt. I'm going to take advantage of being here to do a little sightseeing. Do you have plans for this afternoon?"

"Just some shopping," said Max, "for some new clothes. But we can have dinner tonight if you like. Why don't you drop by at Bernie's, he'd be happy to meet you."

So Béliard dropped by at Bernie's, got along with Bernie, came back the next evening then the evening after that, to the point of dropping by for dinner almost every evening until they eventually got used to his being around.

While Max persisted in his new-found sobriety, it seemed that Béliard, on occasion, gladly yielded to the call of the spirits. One excessive evening, he opened up a little, evoking in a jumble his daily life at the Centre—"It doesn't seem like much, but it's hard working there. You might not think so to look at him, but Lopez can be a holy terror"—and a few episodes of his professional career. As he emptied glass after glass under the worried eyes of Max and Bernie, he pastily alluded to a so-called mission during which he'd had to look after a young woman in dire straits. He was just starting out at the Centre at the time, he laboured to explain, he was in training and it was especially horrible to be a trainee, he assured them, pouring himself another one, they force you to be small, ugly and mean, I who love only what is beautiful and good, but anyway, he'd had to go through that stage. He was clearly delirious.

As the days went by, Béliard, who had started drinking a lot, at times from early in the morning, called in at Boulevard du Temple on a daily basis, to the point where they soon had to take care of him full-time. Bernie arranged for another room for him and they took him for walks, brought him to the Louvre or the Musée d'Orsay, dragged him out to the Mer de Sable amusement park and the Palace of Versailles, made him breathe the clean air of Buttes-Chaumont park. Having no further objection to Max's job at Gilbert's, Béliard accompanied him there every other evening, sitting at a table very close to the piano with an infinitely refillable glass and insisting on loudly giving his opinion of the music afterwards.

But this saturation soon twisted him up, as is sometimes the case, in knots of depression. When Béliard started complaining continuously about his loneliness, despite the fact that he was always on their backs, they searched for new solutions. Bernie even offered to introduce him to girls. Not difficult girls, he hastened to add, but nice, simple girls, the kind you might for example find in abundance at the bar of the Montmorency; but Béliard flatly refused. "My condition," he slurred with a drunkard's gravity, "forbids me." Without making any comment, Max deemed his refusal to associate with mortals rather snobbish.

They went through a difficult period, then, in which Béliard started moaning so much, and so constantly, that they ran themselves ragged trying to help him. They recommended he see someone—but in spiritual medicine he had no confidence. Max, who remembered going through similarly difficult periods, offered to obtain anti-depressants of all kinds, things with lithium that at the time had brought him a little relief, but Béliard refused these as well. He refused everything they suggested. They didn't know what to do with him.

TWENTY-NINE

AND THEN, who knows how or why, the situation gradually improved. After several weeks, Béliard started feeling better. Without going so far as to swing into a manic state, the classic alternative to depression, Béliard's mood took a more serene turn: they saw him begin to smile again, start conversations, even take some initiative. Soon Max and Bernie no longer needed to rack their brains finding distractions for him: he went out all by himself in the afternoons, the entertainment listings in his pocket, and they didn't see hide nor hair of him until it was time for the aperitif—towards which, moreover, he seemed to be practising a certain moderation.

He who, since his arrival at Bernie's, had never lifted a finger to help out with day-to-day life, might now come home carrying—on his own initiative—some shopping for dinner. Truly Béliard was making progress, tidying his bed as soon as he got up, helping with the dishes and the housework, cleaning the bath before leaving the bathroom. Willingly he accompanied Max to the supermarket, nor did he hesitate to change a light bulb or cart the empty bottles to the green receptacle on the corner of Rue Amelot, even without anyone having dared to ask him. The ideal guest: pleasant, cooperative, and so discreet that sometimes Max, coming home late from his job at Gilbert's and consequently rising late as well, didn't see him for the entire day.

On one of those days when Béliard had disappeared—to the Sainte-Chapelle, the Grand Rex, or the Drouot auction house—Max took advantage of his free afternoon to go to the Printemps department store, with the prosaic goal of underwear renewal. Having quickly dispensed with this, he wandered around the store's various floors, with no desire to buy nor any aim other than to pause here and there in front of things for which he had no need whatsoever, a multi-functional shower head, a wide-screen plasma TV, or a panoply of knives—for vegetables, toma-toes, bread, ham, and salmon; for de-boning, slicing, or hacking. All the while, he listened vaguely to the various loudspeaker an-nouncements, which might encourage shoppers to check out this week's bargain on curtains, discounts on household appliances, twenty-percent-off awnings, or Madame Rose Mercœur to please report to the customer service desk on the ground floor.

Of course, it wasn't that rare a first name, but then again, why not? Nor had it been, at the time, Rose's family name, but anyone can get married. In short, it was even more improbable than at Passy or Bel-Air, but he had time to kill, so why not go and have a look? However, the situation was clearly making him nervous, and he advanced discreetly towards the lift without seeming to be in a hurry, with the same detached air and pounding heart as if, having just committed a robbery, he was afraid of being watched— careful not to give himself away by suspicious behaviour under the eye of the surveillance cameras. In the lift, Max continued to display this nonchalant slowness; then, having reached the ground floor, he searched a bit more feverishly for the customer service desk and, once he had found it, believe it or not, this time it was her, it was absolutely her.

It was immediately apparent that Rose, who hadn't changed much in thirty years, in other words, no more than would be expected, had had her nose remodelled, about which Max experienced a wisp of annoyance. We recall that this nose, at the time, might not have been her loveliest feature, but even so, even so. Slightly too hooked, it was so well framed by a perfect face that it ended up being, at the time, all the more endearing. Fine, well, now it had become as pretty as the rest; it was rather a shame, but why quibble? It was, in any case, a handsome job of plastic surgery, wholly worthy of the surgeons at the Centre. As for Rose's outfit, she was wearing at the customer service desk none of the clothes he had spotted the day of his pursuit in the *métro*. It was fairly classic, a camel-coloured cashmere twin set and speckled tweed skirt—Max noted with a pang of emotion that the label of the twin set, having escaped the cardigan, was curled up on the nape of her neck.

She was alone. She appeared to be waiting. Max wanted to go up to her, but she surely wouldn't recognise him—understandable, given the time gone by, not to mention the treatments he'd undergone at the Centre. So she obviously wouldn't identify him, but then again, trying to seduce her with his new name and appearance might even be rather exciting after all these years. Max was dying to approach her, but something held him back; he was embarrassed by his pathetic clutch of shrink-wrapped underpants no less than by the risk, as always, of looking like a . . . although that risk, this time, seemed less likely than it had with the woman with the dog. He nonetheless waited a while, giving his heart time to stop pounding so hard and himself a moment to imagine how he might dare go up and speak to her.

It was then that, from across the store, Max saw Béliard cross the entire length of the perfume department and walk up to Rose, accosting her head-on and without preamble, as if he'd known her for ever. Between Chanel and Shiseido, they immediately launched into an animated discussion, easy and smiling, at the start of which Max, horrified, witnessed Béliard fold the label of Rose's jersey back inside with a familiar movement. After which he seemed to be stressing a point, making his case with eloquence and with the use of gestures, always the same gestures and therefore, no doubt, always the same point. As the conversation went on, Rose for her part showed more and more signs of acquiescence, provoking in return wider and wider smiles from Béliard.

Max could not help starting to walk towards them, like a ghost, but let's not forget that he is only a ghost, then stopped several yards away. As Béliard noticed him at that moment, he beckoned to him to come closer, maintaining his wide smile, come over here so I can introduce you. "This is Paul," he uttered, "a friend of mine. And this is Rose, an old friend I hadn't seen for quite some time." Béliard smiled more and more broadly. "I had almost given up ever finding her again." Max bowed clumsily to Rose, who, as anticipated, gave him merely a slight nod without showing the least sign of recognition. "Well, we'll be leaving now," Béliard announced. "We have a small errand to run."

"Wait just a minute," said Max. "Excuse me, but this person— I think *I'm* the one who was supposed to find her."

"Yes," Béliard said with a cold smile, "I know. I'm perfectly aware of all that, but I'm still the one leaving with her. You see, this is what it's like in the urban zone. This is what it consists of. In a sense, it's what most of you call Hell. So, are we agreed?" he segued, turning back to Rose. "I'm taking you back to the park? My dear Paul, I bid you farewell for the time being."

Standing frozen by the customer service desk, a crushed Max watches as Rose and Béliard proceed towards the glass doors, push them open, and leave his field of vision; then, as if in a trance, he sets into motion as well. Once outside the store, he again spots them walking up Boulevard Haussmann in a westerly direction, but he stops there, follows them only with his eyes, without trying to catch up. At the corner of Rue du Havre, Béliard looks back to give him a little wave, and Max, deader than ever, sees them resume their walk, growing smaller on the receding boulevard before turning right and disappearing into Rue de Rome.

www.randomhouse.co.uk/vintage